OUR GODS HAVE RETURNED

CP HARRISON

Printed in the United States of America.

ISBN
979-8-88945-404-5 (Paperback)
979-8-88945-405-2 (eBook)
979-8-88945-406-9 (Hardback)

Brilliant Books Literary
137 Forest Park Lane Thomasville
North Carolina 27360 USA

Dedication

To My loving wife, who has supported and inspired me throughout the time we have been together. Without her love and support, I do not believe this story would have come about.

PREFACE

For eons, the people of this world have wondered about other life in the universe. They have speculated about a first contact with extra-terrestrial life and how it would happen.

Would it be a peaceful meeting?

Would it be a conquering of our world?

Would they eliminate all human life and take the world for their own?

This story is about a small group of people who have come to a first contact situation and how they handle it. All they know from the beginning is that everything has changed in their world. They know nothing of what has happened to the people and the world outside of their little group. They only know they have survived and must continue to survive.

What they find will differ completely from what they thought was happening. It will change their fundamental views and beliefs about what they all knew.

CP Harrison

CHAPTER

1

"Come on, guys!" Bill Jenson called to his kids. "If you don't hurry, we might as well not bother to go."

He then heard the stomping of feet as both children ran down the hall and came flying downstairs. They both ran by their father and out the door. His wife, Judy, followed them out, giving Bill a smile.

As she went by him, he whispered, "Works every time."

His wife simply smiled over her shoulder as she whispered back, "Not for much longer."

As he continued to walk to the car, he thought about what she had said. It hadn't hit him yet that his kids were getting older, especially his son. They were both still excited about the day trips they took. This year BJ will be a teenager and will look for kids his age to hang out with and forget about his old man. Nancy was only 3 years younger, and he still had a little time with her.

These thoughts would have to wait for another time to think about. Right now, the kids are still excited about today's trip. He started the car and backed out of the driveway. As he put the car in drive, Nancy spoke up with a sarcastically whiny voice, "Where are we going today, Daddy?"

He smiled while concentrating on his driving. He said over his shoulder, "You know how this works. Ask questions to find out."

There were a couple of sighs from the back seat, but no one started the game. Bill began, "I'll start it out." He looked in the rear-view mirror. "We are going to be going west for a little while."

BJ sat there, like he wasn't interested in this game, but Bill knew how he played it. He would listen intently to the questions and answers and then shout out the answer before his little sister. Nancy never caught on to her brother's way. However, she started the questioning, "How long will we be going west?"

It was a good question. Nancy's questions were showing she was now actually thinking about it. Bill thought for a moment, then answered, "I guess about forty-five minutes or so."

She thought for a while, then asked, "What direction will we then go?"

Bill only said, "We will then turn left."

Nancy sternly shouted back, "That isn't a direction, Daddy!"

Her brother leaned toward her and told her in a loud whisper, "If we're going west and turn left, which way would that be?" As he told her this, he used his hand to show her.

 Suddenly she shouted out, "South, we're going to go South!"

Bill turned and gave JB a stern look, and then he nodded.

Nancy again thought about it some, then asked again, "How long will we go in that direction?"

He wasn't sure about it this time, so he could only tell her, "I'm not sure, but less than an hour, I would think."

Glancing in the rear-view mirror, Bill could see both his kids were thinking. He gave them a clue, "I think we are going to be doing a little spelunking."

Now BJ was showing some interest. "What is that, Dad?"

Nancy unfastened her seatbelt and slid forward to whisper to her mother, "Mommy, what does spee..., whatever that was that Daddy said we are going to do?"

Judy turned back and scolded Nancy to put her seatbelt back on. She then smiled at her husband and told Nancy. "Look it up." She then handed Nancy her phone.

Nancy played with the phone a moment the asked, "How is that spelled?"

Judy, being a teacher, was never one to waste an opportunity. She turned and put her arm up on the seat back and told Nancy, "You're going to have to sound it out."

Nancy slumped back in her seat and then told her mother, "I can't even say it."

Bill then said over his shoulder, "Spe...Lunk...ing."

Nancy started by saying, "s."

Judy nodded.

So, Nancy typed that into the phone and then said. "p."

Judy nodded again and said, "Very Good."

Nancy next guessed, "l."

Her mother shook her head and told her, "Before the l, you need a vowel."

Nancy thought about it, and then with excitement, she yelled, "e!"

"Yes, that's right."

Now she guessed the l came next, and this went on until she had most of the word. Then the phone gave it away. Nancy hit enter, and then a list of things came up. After looking at it for a moment, she went to the Wikipedia site. Her mother had taught her that this site usually would help the most. When it came up, she took a little while to read it; however, she made sure she turned the phone away from her brother, who was trying to peek at the screen.

After a couple of minutes, Nancy shouted out with excitement, "We're going to go into a cave!"

Judy smiled at her, and her father said, "Yep, that's right. We're going to Luray Caverns."

At first, there was a flurry of questions, mainly from Nancy, but BJ was a little interested and asked some questions. However, this only lasted for a short time, and then the children quieted down. Nancy was doing something on the phone, and BJ sat there watching out the windows.

When Bill finally turned off the interstate, the interest came back for both his kids. They both kept trying to look for signs and trying to be the first to see them. Unfortunately for Nancy, most of the road signs were on BJ's side of the car. It wasn't long before he yelled out, "You need to turn right at the light."

Bill only took a glance towards him to say, "Thank you."

As he turned back to the road, he saw a slight smile on his wife's face.

It didn't take long before they saw the big parking lot for the caves. It was on Nancy's side of the car, and as soon as she saw it, she yelled out, "Daddy, is that it?"

When Bill nodded, she turned to her brother to rub it in. "I saw it first!" she taunted her brother.

BJ said nothing back to her but sat there looking out of his window, which he knew would make her mad. This activity was the usual way it went on these trips. It was all part of the game they played whenever the family went out.

Bill quickly pulled into the parking lot. As they drove through, his kids looked at all the things there were to do. Nancy wanted to go through the maze, while BJ's priority was to see the old cars. After Bill parked, he let BJ have his way first, since Nancy was so cruel about winning the game in the car. Now, it was BJ's turn to rub it in, and he never passed up an opportunity to get back at his little sister.

They all headed towards the ticket booth. While Bill was getting the tickets, Judy was looking over all the information signs. She, also, was not one to pass up an excellent opportunity. As a teacher, she used this chance to work on Nancy's reading. She had Nancy read the signs while she helped her.

Bill got the tickets, and they headed off to the car museum. At first, BJ face showed little interest with the wagons and such. However, as soon as they got to the cars, he was in heaven. It was a good thing the museum had ropes to keep people from getting too close, because BJ would surely have drooled on some of them.

When they left the museum, it was now Nancy's turn. She was running ahead of her family until her mother called her back. It was only a short walk to the maze, but Nancy couldn't wait. Once they got there, she had to be the first one in, and in no time, she was out of sight. As BJ began, his mother yelled at him, "Try to keep an eye on her! "

BJ looked at his mother with a disgusted look, but smiled back at her and nodded.

Bill and Judy waited outside while the kids tried to find their way through the maze. It took a little longer than Bill wanted for the kids to find their way out again. When he saw them, BJ was right behind his little sister, watching her. When Nancy saw the exit, she ran ahead of him and waited by the gate to tell her brother that she had won.

BJ kept nodding at her, but said nothing. He found out a long time ago that when he didn't respond to her, she really couldn't say anything else. That made her madder than if he had given a response to her. This time, though, it didn't work because her attention quickly turned to the caves.

They took the short walk over to the cave entrance. Nancy stayed with her mother and held her hand as they walked. Once inside, they had a brief wait for the next tour to start, so they walked around the gift shop. It didn't take Nancy long before she started asking for this or that. Each time, Bill told her the same thing, "Wait until after the tour, so we don't have to carry things around down there."

Nancy would go back and put the item that she wanted away. Sometimes she would put it in the back or hide it behind something else so that no one could take it.

Soon they heard their tour group call, and they formed up with the rest of the people. Bill figured there were about thirty people in the group, and the only children were his. The guide introduced herself as Pam, but Nancy was too excited to listen to her. However, Judy yanked her hand when the safety instructions started. She pointed to the young girl talking and said, "You need to listen now."

Nancy tried her best to listen, but she was way too excited. The tour guide finished her instructions and led the group down the stairs into the cave. Now, even though Nancy was very excited, she gripped her mother's hand.

Bill had brought his little camera and began taking pictures of both the kids and the cave. Each time there was a fascinating thing, they would take a group picture. Twice, a younger couple, who were behind them, offered to take the picture so they could all be in it. Every time Nancy would get either in front of or beside her father. She was indeed Daddy's Little Girl.

As the tour was ending, they came into a large open area. The only thing that was really in there was what looked like an organ. Bill had read about this. Gathering his little group together, he quietly explained, "They have put little hammers on the stalactites. As they play the organ, the hammers will hit the right stalactite. Each of the stalactites had just the right pitch."

Quickly, everyone hushed as Pam turned it on. The sound came from all around them. Because of the echo in this room, you couldn't tell where each of the hammers was. After looking around, Bill found a couple, and they all watched as the hammer hit the stalactites. It was such a beautiful sound. However, Bill heard a thump not long after the music started and felt the tiniest vibration under his foot.

Shortly, there were a series of thumps. Some were stronger than others, like whatever it was, is getting closer. It didn't take too long before it sounded very close, and the ground almost threw Bill and his family to the ground. Then the lights in the entire cave suddenly went out. Nancy screamed, but she wasn't the only one. After the initial shock, people started thinking, and soon there were enough lights from cell phones to light up the place pretty well.

As Bill turned on his cell phone light, he found Judy on the floor where Nancy held onto her mother and shook. BJ was standing over them, looking around. He then turned to look around the cave. There were small groups, probably family or friend groups, scattered around the chamber. Soon the emergency lights came on. They were a little better than cell phones, but not by much. Now he searched for one person, Pam, the tour guide. She would be the one with the answers.

After scanning the room, he found Pam squatting down next to the organ. She held her flashlight in both hands, clutched close to her chest. Bill could see how scared their tour guide was. He slowly made his way up to where she was hiding. As he walked up to her, he saw the fear in her eyes. He squatted next to her and asked, "Are you all right?"

She turned to look at him as though she had not even seen him walk up. She didn't speak, but slowly nodded her head.

He smiled at her, and it seemed to relax Pam a little. He then looked back out at the people. Most of them were watching him and Pam. He leaned toward her and whispered, "Do you know what to do when there is an emergency like this?"

Pam nodded again while pulling a little radio out of a pouch on her side. She looked at it as she slowly explained. "When something like this happens, we are to stay where we are until there is a message with instructions from above."

He took the radio as she held it up. When he keyed it and called, Bill was met with silence.

Bill continued to watch her and again smiled at her. This time, she smiled back. As he stood, he returned the radio and offered a hand to help her stand. He again whispered, "I think you should explain things to these people so they will also feel better."

Pan took his hand as she stood, as she slyly nodded an agreement. She then took a couple of shaky steps forward. As she did, the people moved closer to her. It was apparent that she was very nervous, and as she started speaking, it was very soft. Quickly, someone in the crowd called out that they could not hear her. Pam cleared her throat before she began again, "When we lose power like this, we need to stay together and in place until we hear from the office up top. I have the radio here." She then held up the radio so everyone could see it and then continued. "So far, there has been no word. As soon as I hear something, I will let you know. So, the best thing to do is to stay calm and stay together. Someone will contact us shortly."

As soon as she finished, she turned back to him. He thought it might be so she wouldn't have to answer any question. Bill thought she did very well, though she was so scared. Reaching for her, he patted her on the shoulder as he went to step by her. She simply returned to her spot.

Bill went back to his family and found a comfortable place to sit. As soon as he did, Nancy jumped onto his lap and put her arms around his neck. She had been crying, and the tears were still on her cheeks. Her father gently wiped the tears away with his sleeve and slowly rocked with her. BJ sat down beside his mother, put his arm in hers, and laid his head on her shoulder. As Bill watched, Judy looked up at her husband and then back at the children and smiled a motherly, scared smile.

After about an hour, the people became nervous and began talking themselves into a panic. Bill watched Pam and could see she also looked scared and figured she was way above her head in this mess. He stood Nancy up and pointed for her to sit with her mother. Standing, he walked over to Pam, who seemed relieved when he walked up to her. As he squatted down in front of her, he asked, "There's been no word yet?"

Pam pulled the radio out again, and held it up, and as she shook her head, she simply said, "No."

Bill thought about it a little and then asked her, "What is the fastest way out of here?"

She paused for a moment as she looked around, and thoughtfully said, "The only way I know of out of here is to continue on the path until we get back to the stairs." Pointing to a path that went out the other side of the chamber from the one they came in on.

Bill looked the way she was pointing and then back at her. He felt he might need to take over the leadership of this group before she had a meltdown, and everyone would panic. He turned back to her and suggested, "I think I will find another person to go look and see what has happened." However, before he turned away, he added with a bit of a laugh, "I only want to make sure that some idiot didn't forget about us."

Pam returned a small smile as she nodded.

Bill Turn back to the crowd, and in a good command voice, he introduced himself, "I am Major William Jenson, United States Army retired. Please call me Bill." He then paused while everyone thought about it. He then went on, "I am going to go out to find the exit, and I would like to take one or two with me. Are there any veterans or first responders in the group?"

Hesitantly, two men and a woman came forward through the people. Bill stepped down off the organ stand and moved toward the path that led out. As they gathered, he pointed to the first man that got there.

Without needing coaxing, the man spoke up, "I'm Tom Ballard, Sergeant, United States Marine Corps." He was a young man, maybe twenty-five. His hair was short, Marine style, but wasn't quite the buzz cut of a Marine.

Bill looked at him and nodded as he asked, "Are you still active?"

Tom kind of looked down as he replied, "No, Sir, I was discharged about a year ago."

Bill again nodded an acknowledgment to him and pointed to the next man who spoke right up, "I am Navy Corpsman. Petty Officer 3rd Class, Terry Smith." This man was a tall, muscular black man in his twenties.

Bill quickly took an interest in this man. He had a good feeling about a medic in the group. He then pointed to the woman.

She was less military in her response, but still respectful of Bill's rank. "I'm Virginia State Trooper 2nd class, Casey Williams. I am on recovery leave."

Bill looked at her and asked, "Recovery, are you all right?"

Bill figured her to be in her late twenties. She looked at the others as she responded, "I got wounded a couple of months ago in a takedown. I am cleared for duty and report back to work next week."

It impressed Bill with the group he had gathered. He didn't think he could have asked for better. He had a second thought and looked back at Casey. "Are you currently armed?"

She nodded back to him, but offered no more information.

He simply nodded back to her. "We are going to the exit to check things out. I think it has been long enough that we should have heard from someone, and I don't feel comfortable with this situation. I feel something is not right. We should be careful."

No one made any comments, so he went on, "Terry, is it?"

The corpsman nodded.

"I would like you to stay behind for now and check on everyone. I would like a list of names and if there are any underlying medical conditions we need to worry about."

Terry said, "Yes, Sir."

"The rest of us are going to make our way out to the exit and remind them they forgot about us. We need to see what is going on."

He got nods from the remaining two. As he walked, it got a little brighter as the two following him turned their phones on as well.

It didn't take long for the three of them to make it to the stairs. It was a long climb out of here, and they couldn't tell how far it went up as it was out of the range of their lights. However, as they climbed slowly, Bill smelled something. It didn't have any smell other than something burned. However, it didn't smell like wood burning. It was more like a hamburger."

As they went on, Tom quietly asked, "Do you guys smell that?"

They nodded, and both made an affirmative grunt.

Further up the stairs, Bill could make out some light from above. It wasn't a powerful light, and as they got closer, they could see it was streaming in fingers and not a single source of light.

Bill signaled for a stop, and Tom immediately crouched into a defensive position on the left side. Casey stopped and continued to stand. He figured this was because of the difference in training and experience. He motioned for Casey to move to the right and get down, which she did.

The three of them sat there for a few minutes to check things out. It was almost silent at first, except for some popping like wood on a fire, and it sounded like some water running somewhere. Also, the burning smell was much more pungent now.

Bill's instincts were kicking in, increasing the bad feeling he started with. He slowly waved for his group to move forward. When they got to the next landing, they could make out an opening above. There was a lot of debris scattered on the stairs. The opening was about fifty feet farther up and appeared partially blocked, again by debris.

Bill signaled for the other to come to him. He spoke softly, but clearly, "I don't like this. It is not right. I want you two to spread out and move with caution. Trooper, I'd suggest it is time to arm yourself."

He didn't look back but heard her whisper, "Already did."

He signaled them to move forward as he took a careful first step. It was a slow journey to the opening. As they got there, he recognized the exit door was the same door they entered from, and the entire area was demolished. There were openings in the junk around the exit that let the light in, but only a little.

They all stopped together a few steps down from the junk blocking the exit. Slowly, they made their way to the wall of debris. As he looked out, Bill could see about everything within sight was destroyed. A few of the cars were still all right, but most were flaming junks now. He couldn't make out the other buildings, but could see that the entire building housing the entrance and gift shop was in ruins.

Bill could see the blank look on the faces of the others. It was unbelievable that this much destruction could have happened so quickly, and everyone was probably dead.

As he stuck his head back up to look around, something bothered him. He couldn't think what was wrong, but something was not right about this. He continued to look around when Casey spoke up. "Where are all the people?"

That was it. Bill stuck his head back up and looked around again. There was destruction, and there should be dead bodies all around, but nothing. He stood up to get a better look when suddenly, they heard a whoosh of air as if a fast-moving aircraft had flown over. It was from above and behind them. From their position, they could not see it, but they knew it had gone over them.

The three made a quick retreat down the stairs to around the first landing. They gathered in the corner. Even though Tom had taken up a position by the corner, Casey tapped him and showed her pistol. He moved back so she could take up a position.

Tom was a little more than excited when he asked, "What the hell is going on, Sir? What happened to everyone?"

Bill didn't answer right away. Hell, he had nothing new that he could tell them they hadn't already seen for themselves. He thought for a moment and looked at the two of them. "I don't have the foggiest what's going on. We need to get back up there and see if we can figure anything out."

Tom took up a ready stance, but Casey turned around with a question on her face. Bill sat down on the steps and asked, "What is it?"

Casey thought as she spoke, "I'm no soldier, and I've never been in a battle, but I have been in a couple of shootouts, and there are always bodies. Maybe only one or two, but they are always there. What happened to the people who were up there? There should at least be the staff of this place, even if everyone else left."

She was right, and Bill didn't know how to answer her. Finally, he said to both of them, "This is the mystery we are going to have to work out."

With that said, they again made their way back to the top of the stairs. They remained behind the wall of debris as they carefully looked over the destruction. After a while, Bill signaled for them to head back down, when Casey whispered, "Wait, I see something."

Both Bill and Tom were right back up to look. Casey pointed off to the left toward the area where the maze used to be. Soon, they all saw what looked like a man making his way toward the parking lot. They watched as he rushed into the bus parking area where he got onto a school bus.

Bill thought about this, and he was about to stand and signal the man when he heard the bus start. It quickly made its way back to the maze area, and several people came out. Many of them were children.

No sooner than the bus slowed to a stop, a craft of some sort came zooming up. It let out some kind of ray or beam and before he could blink, all the people simply disappeared, and the bus rolled to a stop. The craft then let out another ray, this one was a different color, and immediately the bus burst into flames. The aircraft circled without a sound and then landed in the parking lot a little away from the bus.

Shortly, a creature came out and walked down a ramp that had appeared. At this distance, it was hard to see details about this creature. It was small but humanoid, or so it seemed. It walked over to the bus, and after looking at it a short time, it returned to the craft and took off, about straight up. In nothing flat, it was out of sight.

The three slowly got up and walked back down the stairs. This time, they went all the way to the bottom. When they reached the last step,

Bill sat down and looked at the floor. The others did the same, except they watched him.

When Bill looked up and saw them staring at him, he didn't know what to say. What he saw was nothing like he had expected to see when he got his family together for their day trip. Now his thoughts went to his family and the other families and people waiting in the cave. He didn't know what to tell these two who watched it all happen with him. How the hell was he going to explain this to everyone else?

Bill stood and looked at the other two. His voice was quiet. "We say nothing to anyone until we calm down and think about what happened. Then, maybe, we can explain what we saw."

Casey thought a second and then said, "What are we going to tell them? We can't tell them what we saw, or they will panic."

"No," Tom spoke up, "We have to tell them what we saw. They need to know what we are up against, too."

Bill ended this argument by agreeing with both of them. He cooly told them. "Yes, we must tell them. However, we need to understand what we saw and only then can we try to tell others."

They sat there a moment, and then slowly got up. Without a word to each other, the three headed back to the group in silence.

CHAPTER

2

As the three of them walked back into the organ chamber, Nancy came running up to her daddy, threw her arms around his neck as he bent over to pick her up. "Daddy, you were gone so long I was afraid you wouldn't come back." She cried.

Bill put his hand on the back of her head and held her head down on his shoulder. He swayed with her in his arm and whispered into her ear, "Everything is alright. I am here now."

Nance pulled hard on his neck as she hugged him as tight as she could. While trying to calm her, others from the group of people gathered. Bill squatted down and put Nancy back on the ground. Her mother walked up with BJ, and he gave Nancy's hand to her. Leaning over, he said calmly, "I need to go tell everyone what we saw, and they will probably have a lot of questions, so this may take a little while. You stay with your mother and BJ, and I'll be back just as soon as I can."

As he stood up, Nancy jerked away from her mother and wrapped her arms around her father's leg. Bill reached down and pried her loose and held her by both shoulders, and he whispered to her. "It's alright,

Love. I'll be right up there on the stand where the organ is, and you'll be able to see me the whole time."

Nancy took her head off her father's leg and looked toward the organ. Him telling her this seemed to calm her for now. She went back to her mother as he passed her off to his wife. He headed to the raised platform for the organ. When the others on his little team didn't come up, he motioned with his hand for them to join him up there. Ton and Casey started heading up there; however, Terry stayed back. So, Bill called him out, "Terry, you too. You're part of this group now."

Terry slowly made his way to the front and up onto the platform. He got in line with the others, and they all stood there while they waited for Bill to begin.

Bill didn't know where to start or what to tell them. How do you tell everyone that it looks like aliens have invaded the earth? Finally, he cleared his throat and began, "I took two others with me to check out what happened. It is going to be hard for you to accept. Our world has changed during our time in this cave." A murmur ran through the group. He let it go, and soon everyone was quiet again. He continued, "From what we could see, it would seem that our world is being attacked by what appears to be aliens."

This time, it became more than a murmur. Almost everyone shouted questions at the same time. Bill stood there. After a time, the people realized their questions were not being answered and quieted down. After the questions stopped, he again continued, "We went to the gift shop. That building is now gone." Now, there were no comments, so he continued, "Most, but not all the cars are destroyed and burning in the parking lot. We could not see much past what I have already told you."

Someone in the back shouted out, "Then how can you say it was aliens that attacked?"

Now Bill paused as he glanced at the two that were with him. "Because we saw one."

Again, a murmur ran through the crowd that grew until the people were shouting questions. Bill held his hand up, and after a little, they quieted down again. Now came the hard part to explain, mostly because he still had a hard time believing what he saw, even though he saw it. After a moment, he continued, "We saw some people near what used to be the maze. One of them ran to a school bus and got it started and went to pick up the rest of the people." Again, he glanced at the two, and they were nodding to back up his story. With his attention back to the people, he found his family before he continued. "I was just about to call to the man when some kind of craft flew right over our heads. It came around and hovered over the bus. There was a ray or something. It came out of it, and in the blink of an eye, all the people were gone. It did not kill them right there. They simply disappeared."

Bill watched Nancy and BJ as he told this part. He believed the reality of the things he said didn't reach her. However, BJ held his mother and staring at his father with enormous eyes. His attention returned to the people and continued, "Shortly after that, another ray came from the craft and destroyed the bus. This thing landed, and a creature came out."

It was as if everyone in the room took a breath at the same time. Someone yelled, "What do you mean, creature?"

Bill couldn't tell if it was the same person who shouted out a question before or not, so he went on. "This creature," and he emphasized the word creature, "was a little smaller than us. It had two arms and two legs, and this is where the similarity stops. It had a small head, compared to the body. The body is roughly teardrop shaped. It's skin or clothes or whatever was a grayish blue color." As he described the creature, the room remained silent. He finished by adding, "From our position, this is about all the detail I could make out. The creature went back to his ship and took off straight up, and within a second, it was out of sight."

Now he took a step back to stand with the rest of his chosen group and waited for the questions. In a short time, the shock of this news wore off, and the questions began. Quickly, the questions grew into a flurry. He couldn't tell one from the other. He took a step forward and again held his hands up to quiet them. Shaking his head as he told them, "I can't answer your questions if they are all asked at the same time. I will point to someone, and only that person can ask their question. However, let me introduce the other of my team."

As he introduced each one, Bill motioned for them to step forward. He did not want to face the entire group by himself. The others acted as though they also did not want to answer questions.

He Pointed to a man upfront. This man didn't think long before he asked, "I am guessing the Trooper is armed. Why didn't she shoot this thing before it got away with murdering our people?"

He pointed to Casey and motioned for her to answer. She frowned before taking a single step forward. Bill figured she was not used to this type of situation. Still, she did her best to explain her reasoning. "First, I only have a small pistol with a limited amount of ammunition. Second, this creature was too far away to try for a good hit. Third, we know nothing about them. Even if I got a hit on him, in a kill spot of a human, would it die, or would it simply run back to its ship and use that ray on the three of us?" After she finished, she stood there staring at the man who asked the question.

Quickly, the man lowered his head, showing he realized this was not a very smart question. Casey stepped back as Bill smiled. She had answered the question with an awareness of the situation and force in explaining her decision. He felt this helped the people to feel there might be a little hope.

When he looked back at the group, suddenly, all the hands were down. While he continued to scan the group, a woman's voice asked a question, "What do we do now?" Bill immediately knew this question came from his wife, Judy.

He hadn't had time to think about it. It was a good question, however; he didn't know how to answer it. So, he returned to his military training and dealt with the simple things first. After a moment, he spoke with the same confidence that Casey had shown. "I think the first thing we need to do is figure out what we have here. This cave might be our home for the time being. I don't think these creatures can't see us in here, so I think we will have some safety if we stay here." After no one spoke up, he went on, "I think Pam." he said as he waved for her to join the group on the platform. "Will be key to helping us figure out what we have."

A man shouted out this time, "What we don't have is food and water."

Pam took a step up and said, "There is a lake of clear freshwater. We passed it during the tour. They told me during my training that this water is drinkable. In fact, they said it is filtered so well that it is probably better than the water in your home."

She stepped back, and Bill spoke to answer the other half of the question. "There were some snacks and drinks in the gift shop. We are going to have to see what we can recover from there. This will give us time to plan past that."

After no one else asked any question, Bill finally said, "Let's break up into small family or friend groups and pick one person to attend a council. We will discuss it, and once we have a plan, we will meet again like this and decide what to do."

The people moved away, and there was a lot of small and quiet talk. Bill stopped his group from leaving the stand and announced, "Oh, I forgot to say, you four are automatically in this council group."

The news of this didn't seem to have much effect on any of them. The four of them all acknowledge this news. Bill asked Pam, "Is there some type of an emergency stash of supplies down here?"

The question surprised Pam. However, she recovered quickly. After thinking about it, she nodded as she answered. "There is an emergency supply closet with blankets and medical supplies. Just in case there is a cave in or something."

Tom mumbled, "I'll bet they didn't plan for an alien attack, though."

Most people made a positive reaction to the comment with a laugh, or at least a smile. Bill took this as a good sign. They were still thinking in a positive direction.

Bill motioned for Pam to lead the way and stepped back so she could show them. The group trailed behind her as they went down the same path they had taken a little earlier. This time they went past the stairs and into a small hall cut into the stone. As they reached a door at the end, Pam produced a key and opened the door.

Bill followed her into the room. It is indeed the storage room. It had all kinds of junk in it. All this junk they would have to go through later to see if any of it was useful. Right now, he focused his interest on the stuff in the back corner. As he got closer, he saw there were blankets and lanterns and a couple of cans of fuel. Off to the other side of the room, he saw a couple of stacks of survival food, the kind that could stay good for decades. There were some digging tools and a pile of radios with extra batteries. For now, he had little confidence in the batteries holding a charge. They would need to check it out later.

"Okay," he said to the others, who by now had also come into the room. "We have enough supplies here to last us a little while. Hopefully, it will last long enough for us to make some plans."

While the others searched around the little room, Bill inspected the supplies in the corner. The blankets were the lightweight thermal kind. They wouldn't keep them very warm in the winter. Still, they will do for down here. It wasn't too cold, and most people had brought a light jacket for the tour. The lanterns were the kind you used on camping trips. The question would be, is the fuel still good?

After he surveyed the supplies there, he called the group together. Once they were in a circle, he asked, "Anyone have any ideas?"

Terry spoke up first. "There are a couple of first aid kits here, but not much more than some Band-Aids and Tylenol. We are going to need to find a supply of medicine. A couple of these folks are on some serious stuff."

Bill was glad that Terry had taken his directions a little further and got some medical history on the group. He saw a clipboard hanging on the wall behind Pam. Pointing to it, he asked her, "Would you please hand me that clipboard?"

When she took it off the wall, a pencil hanging on a string came with it. Bill thanked her and began writing as he explained, "We are going to make a list of everything we need on here."

The others nodded as he talked. "The first thing is Meds." To Terry he said, "You'll need to write the medical supplies we need. You're going to be our doctor down here." And he added with a smile, "Doc!"

The others gave a little laugh as Terry got a "Who, me!" look on his face.

Bill's gaze turned to the others, and the laughing stopped when he said, "I wouldn't laugh too much. Every one of us is going to have a job. I haven't figured out past the medical stuff yet."

Everyone in the group wondered what kind of job they would each get stuck with.

They continued to check out the room and found a handcart. When the group left, they loaded up the blankets and a couple of lanterns and a little food and other odds and ends they would need soon. As they were leaving, Pam locked the door again, however before she took a step, Bill asked her for the key.

At first, Pam appeared to be a little worried about giving the key to the emergency supply room to a visitor on tour. However, the reality of the situation came back to her, and she smiled as she handed him the key. Bill still wore his dog tags from the Army. It is an old habit that he felt strange about stopping. He put the key on the chain while everyone watched. No one said anything. It quickly became apparent that he was now the leader of this little group. Now they would go back to see if this was going to hold up with the rest of the people.

On the way back to the organ chamber, Bill gave instructions. To Terry, he asked him to set up an area where people could come if they had a problem. He instructed Tom and Casey that he wanted them to take shifts and watch the stairs. Not that he thought the aliens would come down here so much as other animals. Looking at Pam, he told her, "I want you to come back up the stairs with me and point out all the offices and supply areas and everything you can remember. Eventually, we are going to have to come out of this place. I need to know what we will face."

It didn't take long for them to get back to the group. Some people were waiting for them. There were a couple of ladies that wanted to know if there was a bathroom down here. As they moved into the chamber, more people gathered. This time, Nancy wasn't so terrified that her father wouldn't come back. She ran over and took his hand and gave it a very hard squeeze.

As they got closer, the people were all crowded around. Bill waited until everyone appeared to be a little calmer before he said anything. He wanted to give them some hope and inspiration. He started by telling them, "Okay, folks, we have a fair amount of supplies to hold us for now. If you form a line, we will pass out what we brought back with us. Everyone will get an emergency blanket. They are very light and designed to keep you somewhat warm. We also found some food which we will pass out. These are like the military rations. If you don't know how to fix them, Tom or Terry or I will come around to help you. We also found some cups. We don't have many, so take care of these. You may have to use the same one for quite a while. There are two water jugs we will need to fill. It will take a couple of people to get them filled, so please use the water sparingly. Only for drinking now. We might get a little ripe down here before we get a chance to wash up." That last part got a laugh from some, though most of the women moaned. He continued, "Terry will come around to talk to each of you about any medical conditions and what medicines you take. We will see what we can do about that quickly. Also, let anyone from this group know if you have any ideas about things we will need. Not nice to have things, only necessary things."

Bill finished talking, but the same voice that called the question from the group earlier. The man's voice asked, "Who put you in charge, and who says we have to follow what you say?"

Bill returned to face the crowd. He spoke right up to say, "Instead of hiding in the crowd and yelling out your question, please step forward so I can at least see who I am talking to."

As Bill stood there with his hands on his hips, most people watched as a bearded man made his way to the front. He stopped when he got to the front of the group, yet didn't step up to Bill.

"What's your name?" Bill started in a friendly voice.

The man appeared to be a little nervous and took a moment before he spoke. "Mike." The man replied.

Bill examined this man up and down a little, trying to size him up. He was a short but stout man. It appeared like he was used to working, and clear to Bill that this man had a problem with not being the leader. Bill didn't think he would be too much of a problem if he could get him involved with the team. After taking in as much information as he could about this man. Bill spoke up, "Well, I guess you people put me in charge when no one else stepped up to take the position." Bill didn't wait for a reply. Instead, he motioned for Mike to join him up at the speaking platform. After Mike got to the platform, Bill again talked to the entire group, who had gathered, "There seems to be a question about leadership of this little group. Mike here," he pointed as he continued to speak, "wants to know who put me in charge."

Bill stepped back to stay even with Mike as they both stood there. After a short time with the people quietly talking, one man spoke up. Bill couldn't be sure, but it sounded like an older man's voice. "I don't know who put you in charge. I am certainly glad someone stood up to take the job. We need to have a leader and some kind of organization for this mess."

Before Bill could step up to talk, Mike started talking as he took a step forward. "That's right. We need to organize and start fighting back to chase these creatures off of our planet. We need weapons and a way to find out if there are others, like us, who survived."

Mike glanced at Bill as he stepped back. Bill took his place out in front. Before he could talk, they all could hear a couple more explosions. This time, they sounded very far away. People were getting scared again and mumbling to each other. Bill cleared his throat a couple of times, and everyone quieted, so he said, "I am a retired major from the US Army. I have led a battalion into combat in the middle east. I have been through all kinds of leadership training, training for a situation much like this. When this all started, no one stood up to take charge, so I did. That is what my training told me to do. Mike is right in that we need to organize ourselves to survive. However, to fight back against an enemy we know nothing about, who has weapons that we can begin to understand, would be foolhardy, at best."

Bill turned to Mike as he said the last part, and saw Mike was steaming. Bill immediately kept talking. "We need to see what we have as far as the needs of this group and what this group has to offer in the way of skills. We need to move out of here and try to find more supplies and, yes, weapons. Not so much for fighting the aliens, but for wild animals or other groups that try to take what we have."

Bill finished his talk and asked Mike, "Do you wish to add anything to what you said?"

Mike put his head down and shook it. Bill figured Mike realized he was well over his head in this battle. Bill asked the people, "Is there anyone else who thinks they should lead our group?" When no one spoke up, he continued, "You people will now decide who you want to be your leader. It is up to you if you want Mike or me to lead. We can have a show of hands or a secret ballot." No one said anything, so he added, "Let's go this way first. Let's raise our hands if a show of hands is acceptable. After, we will have a show of hands for those who want a secret ballot."

The people again mumbled so low that Bill couldn't hear exactly what the talk was. However, when the mumbling all stopped, he told them, "Let's have a show of hands for everyone who thinks a show of hands would be acceptable for future votes."

More mumbling, and most of the hands went up. Bill continued, "A show of hands for those who want a secret ballot."

This time, there were only a couple of hands that went up. They were in the area where Mike had come from, and Bill thought this might be his family.

Bill nodded as he said, "Okay, the motion to have a hand-show wins. Now let's have a show of hand for those who want to have Mike as your leader."

Mike didn't even raise his head. Bill counted only one hand raised. He guessed this must be Mike's wife. He asked the same question for a vote for him. This time, everyone else's hand went up. Bill didn't even bother to count. He faced Mike and put his hand out. After a moment, Mike took his hand and shook it. However, still didn't look at Bill.

While Bill still had his hand, he shouted to the group, saying, "I would like to thank you all for supporting me. However, this group still needs leaders, and I think Mike would make a fine addition to the council I am trying to put together."

Now Mike raised his head to see the crowd. There were several cheers and one loud "Hell yes" shouted out. Mike now smiled a little.

Bill again shook Mike's hand and leaned forward to tell him, "In a little while, we will have our first council meeting. Is this alright with you?"

Mike quickly nodded his head and walked down to the group. They gathered around him and shook his hand as he made his way back to his wife, who was smiling at him as she put her arms around him when he got there.

Bill watched for a moment before he headed back to where his family had gathered. As he sat down on the floor, Nancy jumped into his lap. After he wrapped his arms around her, she ask, "Daddy, does this mean you are the boss of the people here?"

"Not exactly, Nancy," he stated. "I am the leader, though a council is a small group of people who will sit down and decide what is needed."

She thought about this for a moment, and asked, "If this council decides things, why do they need you as the leader?"

Now Judy laughed a little, but cut it off quickly as she smiled at him.

Now Bill needed to explain to a ten-year-old little girl how this works. When he glanced at his wife for help, he could see by the look on her face that he was on his own. He thought, and he remembered an acronym used a lot in the military, KISS. This acronym stood for 'Keep It Simple, Stupid' He peered down into her innocent little face. He began to tell her, "There is always a small group of people to decide things. Then there is one that is the leader who the people trust to make the right decision about what to do. One person, the leader, can't possibly think of everything, so a small group helps him, and he will decide which is best."

Nancy's eyes drifted down as she thought about this for a moment. Her father asked, "Do you understand?"

"I think so," Nancy replied, and let the subject drop.

Bill wasn't so sure she understood, and he had other things to think about. He sat there quietly with his daughter on his lap. After a bit, Terry came over, and as he went to squat down, he said, "Excuse me, Boss. I got the info you asked about for the meds."

Nancy glanced up at her daddy when Terry said, Boss. Bill glanced down and said, I'll explain later." He said to Terry, "Gather the others from the council, and we will have our first meeting at the bottom of the stairs."

Terry stood and went off to gather the others. Bill lifted Nancy off of his lap and gently pushed her towards her mother. Nancy said, "But Daddy, he called you Boss."

Bill smiled at her as he said, "Yes, he did." As he smiled at Judy and continued, "Your mom will explain."

Bill now quickly walked away as he heard Judy shout, "Thanks a lot!"

Bill ignored his wife and headed to the stairs. He was the first one there and took a seat on the left side of the stairs about five steps from the bottom, where he closed his eyes and quietly waited.

After about five minutes, the rest of the group began showing up. It took a couple of minutes for everyone to get there and take a seat. As the last person sat down, Bill began, "Welcome to the first meeting of this council. I think we have a talented group of people here who can come up with some good ideas for the rest. I would like us each to introduce ourselves and give a little background history. Mike and I have already given our little talk, so the rest of you go ahead."

Terry didn't waste any time. He did a quick glance at the others and started, "My name is Terry Smith. I am, or was, a medical corpsman aboard an aircraft carrier. After taking a couple of years of college to become a registered nurse, my money ran out, so I joined the Navy for the educational benefits. For my history of training so far, the Navy put me in this job, and I love it. My ship is in port for a refit, so I took some shore time to visit my family. I was driving by here, and I had heard about these caves from some guys on board. I decided to check it out." He paused for a moment. Before anyone else could speak, he added, "I still haven't decided if that was a good move or not."

This got a little laugh from most, but Tom spoke up to say, "I hear ya."

When no one else went, Bill motioned for Tom to continue.

Now Tom appeared to be a little nervous as he slowly started to speak, "My name is Tom Ballard. I was in the Marine Corps. After two tours in the middle east, I decided I had had enough and got out. I was an ordinary rifleman. Nothing special about me." He stopped, and before Casey or Pam could talk, he threw in, "Oh yeah, I was a sergeant and a squad leader." He sat back and threw his arms up to finish with, "That's all, folks."

Again, the last comment got more of a laugh than Terry's previous comment. Bill spoke up before anyone else could say anything and asked Tom, "What have you been doing since you got out?"

Tom hung his head down slightly when he answered, "I've only been doing odd jobs to keep our heads above water. My wife was doing the same thing. I just got accepted as a security guard at the nuclear power plant down by the coast, so we came to see the caves before we moved."

Bill stared at Casey next. However, because she didn't look at him, he called on Pam to be next.

Pam was sitting on the bottom step and had to lean in to see everyone. She smiled as she started, "My name is Pam, ah Pamela. I am attending VPI and took this job during my summer vacation. I now think this was a good idea." Nobody laughed at her joke, so she went on. "I was going to start my senior year in a couple of weeks for a degree in engineering."

Pam stopped and didn't go on. Bill noticed she didn't give a last name, and he didn't press her for it. Now it was Casey's turn. When she didn't speak up, Bill called her out, "Casey?" he said.

She continued to gaze out into the dark of the cave as she started, "I'm Casey Williams, a Virginia State Trooper. I've been on the job for about five years. I usually patrol the northwest part of the state, but I had never seen the caves, so I came today. I should be out there with the other troopers to fight, whatever this thing is."

Bill couldn't tell if it was anger at not being with them or the fact that most of them might be dead and gone that upset her. He decided to get into this later when he knew her better. He felt he needed to ask, "That's fine, Casey. Though now I need to know how you are armed."

She faced him with a little distrust on her face. Finally, she pulled it out to show, "it's a Glock compact nine mil. I have twelve plus one in the gun, and one additional mag with twelve more."

As she put the pistol away, Bill he said, "That's great, for a start. However, we're going to need bigger and better than that, and soon."

She responded, "I have an AR-15 in the trunk of my car. If my car hasn't been blown away by now."

Bill shouted, "That's great, or at least better." He now spoke to Mike. "You're a businessman. What kind of business is it?"

Mike now seamed a little embarrassed for his earlier talk about how good he was. "I run an office cleaning service business in the DC area. I have about a hundred employees working at any given time during the day and night."

This answer stunned Bill a little. He thought Mike might be some kind of big defense contractor or something the way he talked at the group meeting. Suddenly Bill realized it was mostly anger doing the talking before. Now that he had time to calm down, Mike didn't seem to be such a bad guy after all. He made a mental note to watch for this type of anger and aggression from the others in the group as they move forward.

Bill politely nodded to Mike and asked, "Have you had any military training?"

Mike nodded and said, "I did a hitch in the Army as a communication tech."

Bill thought to build him up a little as he told him, "That's great. We are going to need some communication soon. Not only for us to talk as we spread out, but also some long-range stuff. Shortwave or something to see if there are others nearby, we can hook up with."

Mike sat up straighter now. Now he realized he had an essential role in the things around here.

Bill continued with the rest of the group. He assigned Casey and Tom to the security of the stairs. Casey didn't like the idea of having to share her pistol with Tom when she wasn't on watch. However, after a brief discussion, the realization set in that things were not the same as before, and she agreed.

Last came Pam. When Bill called her name, she nearly jumped up off the step. "Pam, I want you to stick with me for a while. You're going to have to show me the layout of everything up top so we can prioritize what we need to get first."

Pam appeared to be excited. Bill didn't think that she had thought this through and that this meant she might have to go outside.

"Okay, Mike," he said as he rubbed his hands together, "For now, Mike, I would like you and Pam, after I'm done with her, to do an inventory of everything in that storage closet. Move the non-important stuff out of there and stash it someplace out of the way. We might find some of it useful in the future."

Mike nodded with his newfound worthiness.

Bill broke up the group, and as they walked back, he said to Pam, "I'm going to grab a bite to eat. After, we'll take a good look around, outside. I suggest you get something to eat as well."

Bill hurried ahead to find his family.

CHAPTER

3

Bill made a quick meal of the emergency rations. He realized they weren't much better than the MRE he had in the Army. However, they had a better selection from which to choose. After they finished eating, Bill found Pam, and the two of them headed to check outside. On his way out, he passed Mike. He thought of something. "Mike," he said as they passed, "could you get other folks to help get water and set up a water station where they can get a drink?"

Mike quickly scanned the area. When he saw the men he was searching for, he ran over to get them before they got away. As he gave them instructions, he waved back to Bill and returned to the task.

Bill quickly caught up with Pam, and they headed to the stairs. Casey was already there at the halfway turn and acknowledged them as they came up the stairs. She had her back against the rail on the far side so that it gave her a good view up the stairs. As he and Pam continued up the stairs, Casey joined them, and the three of them made their way to the opening that was still there.

Bill quickly peeked outside. Most of the fires had burned out, while others were still smoking. It was deadly silent. He could hear the bugs, but that was about all. There were none of the sounds he was used to hearing, so he sat there listening out for a while. He also watched the skies and didn't see any of the alien crafts flying around. He wondered if it was like the Klingons from Star Trek, where the only time you could see their ships was when they were ready to fire.

As they watched, he heard a noise, and they all ducked down behind the debris and remained quiet. After a little while, Bill signaled for the others to stay down, and he crept up to where he could see. After watching for a while, he heard more noise, and this time he could zero in on it. There was a small dog, maybe a puppy, sniffing around. Bill thought he was trying to find food or water.

He motioned for the girls to come up to see. They slowly made their way to where they could also see. Quietly, he pointed to the dog. Pam made a sound, and the dog brought his head up and looked around. Not seeing them, it went back to his search.

After a little while, Bill went back down the stairs to the turn where they had waited before. Pam and Casey quietly followed him, and once there, they all sat close together. In a whisper, Bill asked, "What do you think we should do about the dog?"

Pam was the first to speak up. She talked normally, but with a finger to the lips of Bill, she glanced around and whispered. "I think we need to save the poor thing. It might be a puppy, and I think it's hungry."

Bill and Pam Glanced at Casey. She was a half-second away from tears. Bill put his hand on her shoulder and whispered, "It's okay. We'll save the little thing."

Bill went back to the top of the stairs, alone this time. If things did not go right, he didn't want the other to get hurt. When he reached the wall of junk, he again poked his head up. The dog was still there and randomly moving around, trying to find something to eat. He let out a low whistle, and the dog immediately brought his head up and looked in his direction. Bill kept his head down, but raised his hand above the junk and waved it back and forth. The dog must have seen it and came running to where he was. As it climbed over the top, Bill grabbed him and headed back down the stairs. Once he reached the girls, he told Casey to be ready, and she immediately went to the corner with her pistol drawn.

Bill found the dog was difficult to hold. It was too excited, seeing people and would not be still. Fortunately, he was not barking or making any loud noises. Bill checked the thing over. It appeared to be in good health. There was a collar around its neck and a strap that seemed to be part of a leash. The other end of the leash was gone, and the point where the cut was appeared to be cut with a very sharp knife, and the ends slightly melted together. He handed the dog to Pam and told her, "Keep him quiet and see if you can calm him down."

Pam reached out and took the dog and slowly stroked it. When it rolled over, she gave it a belly rub. This worked, and the dog was now calm.

As Bill watched, the transition was remarkable. He smiled at Pam and gave her a thumbs up. When Bill went back to the top. As he went by Casey, he signaled for her to follow. They both slowly made their way up.

The two of them sat there for a while and watched. Everything was still, and it was getting dark. Bill sat down to think. After a moment, he asked Casey, "Can you see your car, and is it alright?"

Casey moved around a little to get a better angle of where she parked it in the lot. It seemed like most of the cars there were in good shape. After moving back to Bill, she whispered to him, "Yeah, I think so. That part of the parking lot appears to be in good shape. I wouldn't think many cars over there got hit."

After she had finished, Bill thought about it more. They did not know enough to try and venture outside in the dark. He figured this was going to have to wait until tomorrow. He glanced back at Casey to ask, "How much ammo do you have for that AR-15?"

She didn't need to think about it, but answered straight away, "It's together in a go-kit. There are twelve, thirty round mags, a scope, night vision, and a vest."

Wow, she was ready for a fight, Bill thought. It was better than he expected. It would be great if they could get down there to it in the morning. Bill checked to see Casey was still watching outside. He backhanded her on the leg and indicated for her to sit next to him.

She sat down but was keeping her attention on the outside. Bill spoke softly to her as he said, "That was quite an emotional show when we got the dog in. You want to talk about it?"

Now her attention was back on him. He guessed she had not realized that it showed so much. Casey sat there a moment, and as she thought about it, the tears became obvious. She crossed her arm on her knee and put her head down as she spoke. "You remember I told you I was recovering from a shootout?"

Bill answered, "I remember you said something about being wounded, but not specifically a shootout."

Casey continued, "Well, it was a shootout, and I got shot in the leg." She reached down and rubbed her calf as she talked about it. Now she lifted her head and stared at him as she continued, "I was a K-9 officer. My partner was my best friend. When I got shot, he didn't listen to me and attacked the perp to protect me. The perp got three more rounds off, and two of them found Jojo. He was dead before I could even crawl to him. The perp got away, but later, he was shot dead when they tried to arrest him again."

Bill knew exactly what she was going through. He had several dog handlers in his units, and whenever one of them lost their partner, they had a tough time.

Casey continued with her story. "That night, it was like my heart was pulled from my chest. Tonight is the closest I have been to another dog since that happened. I don't know that I could go through anything like that again."

Bill continued to nod as she spoke. He was sure she had gone through all kinds of counseling and that by the doctor's definition, she was fit for duty, but from experience, he knew better. Those soldiers he knew were never the same as before.

Bill stood and patted her on the shoulder and quietly told her, "Your secret is safe." And as she watched, he stood and motioned for her to follow him back down the stairs.

When they got back down to where Pam was waiting, it was already dark. Bill could barely make out Pam sitting with the dog in her lap. The dog appeared to be sleeping. However, as soon as they sat down, it again became active. It first came to Bill, and he pet it for a couple of minutes, and after it went to Casey. She did not pet it, even when it tried to get under her hand. She ended up pushing it away. Pam glanced at Bill with a big question mark on her face. He shook his head to show not to ask.

The dog finally went back to Pam and laid down. As she pet it, she announced to everyone, "I think I'm going to name her Sadie. It reminds me of an aunt I used to have. "

Bill's head came up quickly and replied, "Her?"

Pam jokingly snapped back, "Yes, contrary to what you think, all dogs are not good boys!"

Bill laughed at that, but when he saw Casey, she only gave a slight smile.

After sitting a little longer, Bill and Pam got up to leave. Before he left, he waited until Pam was a little way down the path. He asked Casey, "Are you going to be okay?"

She told him, "Sure, I go through this every time I see another dog. It will pass."

As he was leaving, he stopped to ask, "How long are your shifts?"

"We'll switch at midnight. We figured that during the day, there are enough people to monitor things."

Bill gave a thumbs-up as he left. He quickly caught up with Pam. The little dog, Sadie, was tagging along right beside her. This little girl might bring much-needed joy to the folks down here. If a little puppy could survive, it may give them hope their families might also have made it through.

When they came into the organ chamber, Nancy came running to her dad again. However, as soon as she saw the puppy, she ran around him to see the dog. Bill now figured he knew where he stood in the pecking order around here.

Nancy dropped to her knees and played with the dog. Pam stood over them to make sure neither one got too carried away with the play. Nance asked Pan, "What's his name?"

Pam immediately thought, "Like father, like daughter." She answered with, "First he is a she. And her name is Sadie."

Nancy tried to pick Sadie up to hug her, but Sadie was too excited for any of that. More people had gathered to see the dog, and everyone wanted to pet her.

Bill watched for a moment, but soon headed over to where his family had set up camp. Judy came up and hugged her man. BJ moved over to let his father have the best seat around. A nice flat spot on the floor. As Bill got comfortable, Judy brought a cup of water for him.

He gulped it before he realized it had a funny taste to it. It wasn't an unpleasant taste, He didn't expect it.

Judy gave a little chuckle and told him, "That's better than the first drink I had. I tried only to sip, and that didn't work. It's worse when you sip it. It's best to just bottoms up."

Bill could not imagine it was worse than gulping it down, but he had learned over the years not to debate issues of opinion with her. Hers were always right and his wrong.

He ended it with, "Not too bad. Could be much worse."

She had set up a lantern near their spot. There were two more scattered around. All of them were set to low to save fuel. Judy told Bill that Mike had arranged it that way.

Bill thought about it for a minute. Mike might not be the sharpest tack around, but he knew a few things about managing and surviving. Bill took water and mixed up a pack of the food. It was a chili, he thought, and wasn't too bad.

After eating, Bill tried to relax a little; however, people would come around. A few would wave or say hello and continue on their way. Others would stop to talk. The subjects ranged from what he thought the aliens wanted with them, to if the dog survived, could people also survive? Most of the time, he tried to give them an answer that he thought they wanted to hear.

After a while, the people settled down, and everything became very quiet. Occasionally, Bill could hear a very distant explosion, but nothing was close. Nancy had fallen asleep with her head on his lap. Judy got curled up in a little ball against the wall, and BJ was asleep not far from her. It did not take too long before sleep overcame him, and Bill finally fell asleep.

The morning of the second day of their new future began not too differently from other days. The Jenson family gathered for breakfast, even though it was a much different breakfast than the day before. Also, this was not the Jenson's kitchen. However, for each member of the family, the differences mattered little. They were together.

Not long after they sat down to eat, Tom came in from his watch. He appeared to be exhausted. Tom still had Pam's pistol in his belt. Bill called him. He came over and sat down next to the family.

"How did the watch go? See anything happening?" Bill asked, after Tom got a little comfortable.

Tom had a bit of a vacant stare, but his answer was clear enough. "I think I saw a couple of those ships fly by on the horizon. They were too far away, and it was too dark to say for sure. I also heard explosions in the distance. They sounded like they might be coming from the east."

Bill listened as Tom spoke. After he finished, Bill leaned over to say, "Good man. Now get some sleep. We will see you later today. We have the watch now."

Tom turned his head to look at Bill with empty eyes. After a moment, he slowly stood up. Before he walked away, he took the pistol out of his belt and handed it to Bill as he asked, "Will you give this to Casey? I don't think I can stay awake long enough to find her."

Bill carefully took the pistol from him, saying, "Sure thing. Don't worry about it. I'll find her for you."

Tom waved as he walked away.

Nancy came over to her dad and watched as Tom walked away. After a little, she turned to her dad and asked, "What's wrong with that man? Is he going to be alright?"

Bill watched as Tom found his wife and a place out of the way to lie down. Chuckling a little as he answered his daughter, "Yes, he will be alright. He had to stay awake all night to watch outside so we would be safe down here. He is super tired."

Nancy stood there a moment longer, and finally said, "Oh." She headed toward where Bill thought Pam was. He knew she would get to the puppy first thing in the morning.

Casey and Terry stopped in to say good morning and ask what Tom had said. Bill passed on the report, and Terry dropped his head, saying, "This can't be happening. It must be a dream."

Casey spoke to add, "This isn't a dream; it's a damn nightmare."

As Judy stepped up, she heard what Casey said and threw in her two cents with, "Amen to that."

Bill finally did the introductions, and there were the usual niceties and handshakes. He pulled Casey's pistol from his back and handed it over to her, telling her, "Tom was dead on his feet when he finished the watch. He asked me to return this to you. I took it before he passed out."

Casey took her pistol back and immediately cleared and checked it, put the clip back in and racked the slide back. She made sure the safety was on before she put it back in her holster. She eyed Bill with a what's next look.

Bill gave an approving nod and asked, "Y'all ready to take a little walk outside?"

Casey said, "Hell yeah."

Terry quietly showed he was ready.

Bill grabbed his cup and took a drink. After he finished, he almost crushed the foam cup, but quickly recovered and handed it to Judy and asked, "Would you please put this someplace safe for me?"

Judy took the cup and leaned in to kiss him. With a wink, she went back to their area.

Bill turned to the others, who both had smiles, and shyly glanced at the ground.

"Alright, let's go," Bill said as he stomped past them. Behind him, all he heard was a little giggle.

As he got closer to the stairs, it started to get a little cold. When he reached the stairs, he walked up to the turn, where he could feel the cold air coming down the steps. Going back down, he went down the hall, telling the other two to follow him. He headed to the storage room and, once inside, went straight for the blankets. Handing them out to Casey and Terry, he told them, "We might need these this morning. It feels pretty cold out there, and I don't know about you guys, but I didn't bring a jacket with me yesterday."

Casey mentioned, "I got a real nice State Trooper jacket in my car."

Both Bill and Terry turned their backs to her as they broke out the blankets. It did not take long before they were ready for the outside. Bill led the way up the stairs. As before, he stayed behind their wall of junk to peek around. After about a half-hour of watching and seeing nothing, Bill slowly stood up and made his way over and around the debris blocking the entrance. The others followed him out.

It was slow going as they checked all the stuff scattered around. There were boxes and junk from the store thrown all over the place. They found the area where they sold most of the snacks. Much of it was still there and seemed to be still eatable. Bill picked up a candy bar. Other than being a little melted, it appeared to be okay. After checking, he took a bite, and while still chewing, he motioned to the others to try.

They continued to walk around the gift shop area. Other than the snacks and drinks, there was not much in the way of useful stuff to be found. It was Terry that first asked the most crucial question, "Where are all the people? This place should be full of bodies."

Both Bill and Casey indicated to Terry that he was right, and all three of them stood there scanning the area. They were now searching the same stuff they searched at before. However, before they were not looking for anything in particular. Now they were searching for something that was simply not there.

Casey spoke first. "They must have used that same ray on everyone in here, like the people trying to get on the bus yesterday."

Bill remembered Terry was not with them when they saw the people vanish. He tried explaining it to Terry, who stood there in disbelief.

Bill could not help him, though. He had enough trouble believing what he had seen. He went back to searching. Although they never left the ticket area and gift shop, they could see the area around the park. Most of the homes and other buildings they could see were still standing. However, many were burned to the ground with a few more still burning. There are a lot of smoke columns on the horizon in all directions. Bill guessed it was more buildings burning.

As he was scanning the sky, trying to guess what had happened, he saw a tiny spot among the few clouds. He watched it for only a second. He could see it was quickly getting bigger. Glancing back to the cave, and a quick calculation in his head, he realized this thing would be on top of them before they could get back to the safety of the cave. He quickly shouted at the other, "Something is coming! Get down among the junk and cover up with this blanket and hope they don't land to check it out."

Bill quickly found a spot next to him, and after he got down, he spread the blanket around and tried to make it look like the other garbage scattered everywhere. Before he put his head down, he again shouted to the others, "Try to make the blanket is like a part of the trash and stay still until I give the all-clear."

Bill did not wait for a response that he knew wasn't coming. He slipped his head under the blanket, tried to curl up into a ball, and held as still as he could while still breathing.

Bill thought he heard the same rush of air he had heard yesterday when they first saw the other machine. For a long time, it was silent, but Bill noticed he could hear a very slight humming. It appeared to be moving around and stopped for a little while. Bill couldn't tell if they were landing or searching. After what seemed like an eternity, he heard the rush of air again, and the hum was gone. He was thinking and praying the machine had gone away the same way the other one did yesterday. Bill slowly moved his head enough so only his eyes could see. Moving nothing but his eyes, he peered around as best he could. Seeing and hearing nothing, he slowly brought his head out more to see more. Bill was mainly scanning the sky, but got a good peek at the grounds. There was nothing. Finally. He sat up, and after doing one more check, he called out, "All clear, you can come out now."

Slowly the other two uncovered and looked around, as he had done. Bill, however, was too busy watching the sky to notice. He kept watching. The other two came to where Bill had hidden and stood there, waiting for instructions. Bill needed time to think so he could put his entire head into this problem. Finally, to them he said, "Let's head back to where it is safe. I need quiet time to think."

They gathered up their blanket. As they walked past the snack area, all three of them put as much of this junk in their blankets as they could, pulled up the corners. Throwing the sack over their shoulder, and without a word between them, they went back down the stairs into their sanctuary.

After waiting to make sure nothing was following them, they headed down the path to their new home. When they emerged into the chamber, all the talking stopped, and everyone watched them. The three made their way to the organ platform, but did not go up the ramp this time.

Bill had them place their sacks on the floor, and once most of the people had gathered, they opened the blankets. There was a small round of applause as everyone stepped up to see the loot. It did not take the two kids long to realize what happened when they both grabbed a couple of things. BJ grabbed a soda and two bags of chips while Nancy picked out her favorite candy bar and took two of them. All the people began laughing and pointing things out for the kids. However, when the children finished and left, everyone stood there staring at it.

Finally, Bill had enough. He shouted out, so even the people who hadn't gathered could hear, "Help yourselves. Just make sure there is enough left for everyone to get some."

When he finished talking, Bill reached down, picked up a little pack of cookies, and headed over to his area to be with his kids. As he was leaving, the people moved up and picked through all the stuff.

Bill found Nancy and BJ in their area, enjoying the spoils of the trip outside, but Judy was not there. After a quick scan, he found her helping people get their snacks. She soon joined him, and together they ate in peace.

Shortly, he laid down and went over everything that had happened today in his head. Bill still wasn't able to get his thoughts together because everyone kept walking by and stopping to say hi or to ask questions. Finally, he got up and went back to the stairs to sit and think in peace.

Now he could focus. He had about a thousand different questions running through his head, but it all came down to why. And there were a lot of reasons.

The biggest why would be, why are they attacking earth? Bill thought about that for a moment. However, he could not think of a reason for this kind of unprovoked attack. It suddenly dawned on him that the big reason had no answer he could understand right now. He had better work on the petty reasons to build up knowledge first. He was started with today. There were a couple of why's that concerned him. First, why did that ship come to this spot while they were out there? Were they able to somehow detect his people once they were out of the cave? Next, why didn't it attack the three of them while they were right there? It would be nice to think his camouflage worked and appeared so natural to the aliens. No, he figured it wasn't that good. Could they not see them for another reason? He figured he was going to have to think about that one more. However, this seemed to be the only why he had a chance of figuring out right now.

Bill decided to put this before the council to get more ideas about it. He felt a little better now that he had a plan and direction to get started on. Now, he relaxed and listened to the silence of the cave until he fell asleep.

After a quick nap, Bill again joined the group. Nothing new was going on. People were wandering from group to group with a bit of chatting. Bill found Mike talking to some other men in a small group. As he walked over, all the men stopped talking and stared at him.

"Gentlemen." He said with a quick nod to everyone. Directly to Mike, he continued, "Mike, I think it might be a good time to get the council together. What do you think?"

Mike didn't think about it for long before he replied, "I think they are ready. A couple of these men are on the council." As he said this, he pointed to the group, but none of the men in particular.

Bill said, "Great, let's get together and start getting this group moving. I would like to meet at the bottom of the stairs down that path." He pointed to the path they always went down to get to the stairs. He continued, "You gather the group, and I'll meet you there in about fifteen minutes."

Mike peered at him with a question on his face, so Bill leaned in to quietly told him, "I need a couple of minutes to visit the men's room."

Mike smiled at him and went to get the rest of the council together.

After a stop at the men's room, Bill found his four people and told them about the meeting. Before he could leave Pam, she asked, "What should I do with Sadie?"

After a quick thought, Bill told her, "I don't want her at the meeting. I think she would be a little too disruptive. Maybe you could get BJ or Nancy to watch her."

Pam glanced down and stroked Sadie a little and nodded her reply to him.

Bill headed for the stairs. As he got closer, he could hear a few people talking. It was small talk about their new life; however, Bill could hear a few people talk about going outside to see for themselves. When he came into sight, all the talking stopped. As he approached, Bill gave a little wave as he climbed a few steps up the stairs. Standing there, he held his hand out, indicating for the people to sit, and politely said, "If you please have a seat, we'll get this thing started." As he was sitting, he added, "We have much to talk about."

There were a couple of mumbles of agreement from the group as the people found a place to sit. Bill was sitting on the highest step to show he was the leader. Nobody challenged it, giving him a good feeling about this group. Scanning the people, he began by saying, "I would like to thank you for agreeing to help lead this group. I think we should start by introducing ourselves. You heard my introduction for the election as well as Mike there." he asked, "Mike, is there anything you would like to add to your description of yourself?"

Mike was a little taken aback by the question, and in a somewhat uncomfortable tone, he answered, "No, I think I said everything then."

"Okay," Bill said as he clapped his hands together. He went to the man sitting to his left to say, "Let's start with you and go around the group."

That man stood to say, "My name is Jim Taylor. I was down here visiting my son, and my wife always wanted to see the caves. I thought yesterday was a good day to do that." This got a couple of little remarks, but he continued, "I was a lawyer up north. However, now I am retired. My wife worked as my secretary, so she retired when I did."

Jim quietly sat back down and glanced at the next person.

The next person was a middle-aged lady. She also stood and started, "My name is Susan. I work in the school cafeteria in a little town northwest of Washington. A couple of my friends and I decided to take off for a couple of weeks and make a road trip. We've been stopping at different places, and this place was next on our list."

Finished, she politely sat down.

These introductions went around the group. When it came to one of Bill's chosen ones, they went by only saying their names. When it got back to Bill, he didn't stand as he began. "Folks, I don't need to tell you that life as we knew it is over. We are now in survival mode. Not only for our lives, but for the entire human race." He let that sink in for a minute before continuing. "There are so many unknowns about this situation. I don't know where to begin. I decided that the big picture of why they are attacking and killing everyone is too much for us to think about right now. We need to start with getting ourselves set up. We know this cave is safe, and I would suggest we stay here."

There was a slight murmur that went around, but when Bill put up his hands to clarify his meaning, "When I said to suggest, I meant to suggest. This group is here to develop ideas and strategies for our survival. Once we have thought about something, we will take it to the entire group, explain as best we can, and vote to decide."

When he stopped, no one spoke up. So, Bill continued, "The first thing we need to get is supplies." There were grunts and nods. "When I say supplies, I am talking about food, medicine, clothes, weapons, and two-way long-distance type of radios."

"How are we supposed to get these things when we can't even go out?" asked one man. Bill could not remember his name and figured it would take a little while to get to know everyone. He let this set a little while everyone thought about this. Finally, Casey spoke up. "I guess we are going to have to take a chance to gather supplies for the rest."

Bill glanced around the group. Most of them held their heads down, thinking they might get chosen for this job. Bill got a slight grin on his face before he spoke. "I have an idea about that." Now everyone was staring at him, so he continued, "I'm not so sure they can see as we do. I believe they can see heat. The heat from our bodies, heat from the cars, once started, and warm-up, any kind of heat source. When they detect something that doesn't look right, they come down here and check it out. I believe that happened to the bus and the people we saw. I don't know if they saw all the bodies and started down here or if it was when that man started the bus."

Mike asked, "Are you sure about this, and how sure?"

"No, I'm not very sure at all. It is only my theory."

Again, the people were not helping with ideas. Bill let out a sigh and now spoke slowly. "I guess one or two of us are going to have to prove this theory. When we were outside checking around, we saw one of those ships coming. We took cover by putting the blanket over us and acted like the junk all around. My face was covered so I couldn't see, but after a little, I could hear an incredibly low hum from that machine."

Terry now spoke up, "I heard it too, but I didn't realize it was from the machine."

Casey added, "Me too."

"At first, I didn't realize it was from the machine, either, but I heard it moving around, and I knew." Bill went on. "It moved around, and

I could swear it hovered right over me. I don't think it saw us through those thermal blankets."

Now the people were thinking. Jim, the lawyer, stood up to talk. "We are going to have to have someone out there to see if your theory holds up."

As he sat down, Bill asked, "Are you volunteering?"

Jim stop halfway through sitting and stood back up to definitively say, "No sir, not me. I'm too old for this kind of thing."

Bill laughed as he spoke. "I'm sorry, Jim. I was merely joking with you. And, by the way, this isn't a courtroom. You don't need to stand every time you want to say something.

Jim glance over the group and the smiling faces. Back to Bill, he said, "Just old habits."

Bill asked, "Anyone else have any ideas?"

The silence was deafening. Finally, after a long while, Casey spoke up to say, "We are going to have to have someone go out there and lay down to see if those things come." Before she finished, she quickly added, "And hope your theory is right."

There were a lot of sounds of agreement with her last statement. Bill smiled, but then got serious. "That is why I am going to be the one that goes out. I can't ask any of you to do something like that."

Now no one spoke for a long time. The only other lady in the group spoke up. Again, Bill could not remember her name, but he thought she said she was a manager. She was already standing but took a step towards the middle of the group to speak. "That is all fine and dandy. However, it won't prove anything unless they happen to fly over this one little parking lot in the whole world. If they don't show up, it simply means they didn't see you, but not for the reason you're trying to prove."

Yep, she was right, Bill thought. If they don't show up, it doesn't prove that they didn't detect his body heat under the blanket."

Mike now spoke up, "If my car is still in one piece, I have a remote starter. You could lie out there a while to see if they come. You can start my car and see how long they take to get here." Mike held out his keys and added, "It's not like I'm ever going to drive it again."

Bill thought about it for a minute before he stood up to say, "I think that will work fine." After waiting a minute, he asked, "Does anyone have any other ideas?"

Again, the room was silent. Bill took two steps down the stairs and stopped to announce, "We will do it this afternoon." When no one said anything, he added, "When we meet again, I want to hear a lot more from all of you. You were chosen, by whatever means, to represent your group. Talk to your people. See if they have any ideas. Come back here, ready to get down to work and start moving on with our survival."

Bill waited while everyone else filed out of the area before he headed back. His chosen few were still hanging about. When he moved, they moved to block his path. Bill could not be sure it was an intentional block or only happened that way, but he couldn't go by them without pushing someone out of the way.

Tom took a step toward him before he spoke. "Sir, you can't be the one to go out there. You are our leader, and the entire group needs you. I will be the one to go out there and test your theory."

Before he could answer, the other two stepped up beside him and added their support to what Tom had said. Bill took a step back and peered into each of their faces. He saw the determination in their eyes. Unable to speak, he merely held the keys to Mike's car out for Tom to take and lowered his head.

Back in the area, the word had already gotten out. First, Nancy came running over and locked onto her dad's leg and crying, "Daddy, you can't go out there. You will die."

Following her were Judy and BJ, but he held up his hand before they could say anything. Talking calmly, he said, "There was a last-minute change of plans. Tom is going to go out instead of me."

Judy cupped her hands over her mouth to hide the relief she was feeling, and that Bill saw in her eyes. BJ stood beside her, and Bill thought he did not understand the situation from the blank expression on his face. Nancy, however, understood. She asked, "Daddy, does this mean you're not going out there?"

Bill bent down and picked her up, and when she was face to face with him, he said, "Yes, Sweet Thing, this means I am staying in here."

Nancy threw her arms around her daddy's neck and hugged him so tight he had to put his hand under her arm so he could breathe."

As he started walking back to the family area, he told Tom, "Get some food and hit the head. I don't know how long you'll be out there, but once you're there, you can't move."

Tom shot him a thumbs-up as he went to get food.

Bill headed to his family area and grabbed a little food for himself. As he was eating, Nancy came over and sat next to him and snuggled up against his side. Her big eyes stared up at him, and she asked, "Daddy, what is going to happen to us? Are we going to stay down here forever?"

Bill did not answer right away. How could he answer her when he could not answer the same questions he had been asking himself? However, how could he answer her without scaring her or without lying? He glanced away to the crowd of people and told her the simple truth, "I don' know, sweetheart. We need to stay down here for now because we know we are safe here. Once we find a way to go outside without being seen, we will see what happens."

Nancy gazed back down and slowly nodded her head. She didn't say anything more, so Bill couldn't be sure she understood what was happening. After a little, Nancy quietly got up and walked back over to her mother. After she sat down with her mother, Judy looked back at Bill and held her finger to her mouth to tell him to be quiet.

He knew what she was saying. Judy wanted everything to be peaceful so that Nancy could think in her way. Her mother could answer her questions so she could understand. Bill could never have a serious talk with his daughter. He found he could not bring it down to her level, so he always passed it off to Judy. Sometimes she didn't know or understand things and would ask Bill. He could explain to her, and she could then bring it to Nancy at her level of understanding.

Shortly, Tom and Casey came over. Both had blankets. Bill must have had a curious face. However, before he could ask about it, Tom spoke, "Sir, we decided that if this test works, we will head over to Casey's car and grab her gear while we can."

Bill was thinking as Tom spoke. After he thought it through for a moment, he said as he stood up, "Good idea. Are you both ready?"

Casey and Tom showed they were ready.

As Bill started moving toward the stairs, he said back over his shoulder, "Okay, let's get to it."

The three of them were starting down the path to the stairs, Terry ran up. As he got close to the group, he held up a first aid kit, and in a low voice, he said, "Just in case."

Bill nodded approval, and Terry fell in at the end of the line. When they got to the bottom of the stairs, Bill stopped and motioned for everyone to sit down. After sitting, Bill lay out his plan. "Tom, I want you to go out into the parking lot and get about twenty-five feet away from Tom's car. Spread out the blanket and lay there for about an hour or more." Bill checked for understanding before continuing. "If nothing happens by then, I want you to start his car and stay very still. I believe this is when our friends will show up."

Terry asked, "What happens if they don't show up.?"

Bill had to admit to himself that he hadn't thought about that in his plan. After a moment he responded, "If they don't show up in two hours after you start the car, then shut the car off and head back this way, while keeping under the blanket."

Tom showed he understood, but then Casey asked, "What about me?"

Bill explained, "I would like you to follow Tom out and set up on the edge of the lot where you can still hide in the junk piles. This way, we can tell if they simply can't see him or if they can't tell the difference between you and the garbage." He paused to see if this plan would work for them; however, he added, "Of course, if they can see both of you then…" Bill let it trail off because they all understood what the outcome would be if the aliens saw them.

Tom laughed a little as he simply said, "Yeah, right."

Casey didn't even react to the comment. She simply picked up her blanket and got ready to go out.

Bill only had one radio he took from Pam. While the others got ready, he went to the supply room and got two more radios. Once he was sure they all worked together, he gave one to each of his adventurous pair.

Tom and Casey headed out. Once at the top of the stairs, they stopped to get the blankets ready and wrap themselves up. They slowly made their way through the junk. Once at the edge of what was the building, they stopped to scan around. Past this point, the two of them separated. Casey went to a brush-covered area next to the parking lot. Tom continued on his way into the parking lot.

As Tom got to the cars, he stopped again. After checking around, he pulled out the keys and pressed the panic button to find out where Mike had parked his car. A car horn slowly honked, and as soon as Tom figured out which car it was, he pressed the button again to kill the horn. The car was near to where he was, so Tom went a little further to an open area, and got down under his blanket.

Bill and Terry were watching both of them and the sky at the same time. They had moved into the gift shop area to get a better all-around view but still stayed in the junk that used to be the gift shop.

Bill told Terry to set up in one spot, and he moved to another area a little away. He didn't want the two of them to be together. Once they were ready, Bill got on the radio and called, "Radio Check."

Casey answered first, "Good, all clear."

Tom answered, "I'm good, and all appears to be clear."

Bill did not reply to either of them. He wanted to stay off the radios as much as possible.

Now the waiting began. It was a warm day, and Bill felt sorry for Tom and Casey. He and Terry were still in the shade, but those two were both out in the scorching sun and covered by blankets. Bill wished for a pair of binoculars. Not only to watch his two people, but also to scan the sky. He was thinking it would be almost impossible to see one of those ships coming again. It was by pure luck he saw it the first time. Not knowing what direction they would come from also lessened the odds they could see it, but Terry and he continued to try.

After a while, Bill checked his watch. It was slightly over an hour since Casey and Tom had gone out. He gave one last good scan of the sky. When he convinced himself it was clear, he let out a low whistle. The whistle was the prearranged signal for Tom to start the car.

He focused his attention on the parking lot. Shortly he heard a car starting. Zeroing on the sound, Bill found the car that must be the one that Mike had described. Bill quickly reminded everyone, "Keep perfectly still, no matter what."

The alien aircraft was over the parking lot in less time than it took when Bill and the others got caught on the outside. Bill and Terry stayed down, but Bill could steal a peek now and then through a little gap in the junk. The craft hovered over the car, and in a short time, the ray from the aircraft destroyed the car.

Bill ducked back a little when the car exploded, yet continued to watch the alien craft. It continued to float around the car, like it was searching for something more. After the second circle of the parking lot, it took off. However, this time it didn't shoot straight up. It left in the direction it had come. It was out of sight behind where Bill was, so he couldn't tell if it was truly gone or not. He keyed up the radio and simply said, "Stay put."

After about a half an hour, Bill moved out from behind the debris where he was hiding. He slipped to the side of what remained of the building where he could watch in the direction the craft went. It also allowed him to scan the sky for a long time. However, couldn't see anything. On the radio, he told the others, "It looks to be all clear, but remember to keep covered up as you move."

A moment later, he could see both Tom and Casey moved. Slowly, they moved towards the other part of the parking lot where Casey's car was. They kept their distance from each other as they moved. It was a smart move. Suppose there was a little body heat escaping from under the blanket, and they were close together. In that case, it might be enough to attract the attention of the aliens.

Tom and Casey made it to her car and gathered the stuff she had. As they made their way back, Bill moved back into the tunnel that leads to the hideout. Terry was already waiting there. He had a little time to absorb his first encounter with the aliens. He was excited, he talked about it to everyone as they came in.

Bill sat there waiting for the other two to get back while Terry went on about the events that had happened. Casey was the first one to come over the wall of junk and quickly followed by Tom.

Casey already had a mag in the rifle, and Bill guessed she had already chambered a round. Tom carried the rest of the gear in the bag. Bill saw she had also grabbed her jacket while they were there. He commented on her needing to guard against people trying to steal the nice jacket. She just showed the rifle and said, "That wouldn't be wise."

The others laughed, and Bill motioned for them to move down away from the opening. When they got to the bottom of the stairs, Bill sat down, and the others gathered around him. He started by asking, "What do you think?"

Terry shouted, "That was amazing!"

Bill hung his head down and smiled, but when he brought his head back up, he was more serious. "Yes, it was, but I was talking about our experiment."

Terry sat down and said, "Oh, yeah."

Tom jumped in, "I think this proves the theory. They only came in after the car started and were there within a few seconds."

Bill shook his head as Casey added, "Yes, there were there quickly, but remember the last time with us caught outside. It took a long time, relatively, for them to get here."

Bill thought for a moment, and added, "This is true, and they came in from a different direction. Also, this time when they left, they didn't fly straight up."

Casey slowly asked, "What do you think this means?"

Bill didn't immediately answer her. He thought for a little, before he told them, "I think this tells us a couple of things. First, they are not watching us from space. It tells me they have patrols. It might be area patrols, or it might be roving patrols. We are going to need to be careful as we begin to move out of here."

Tom now added his thoughts, "Yes, but this proves we can move around without them detecting us."

Bill shrugged his shoulders and gave a single nod to answer Tom, but added, "Maybe. We will still need to be very careful when we go out."

This comment got a round of agreements from everyone. Bill stood but stopped to say, "I still feel, deep down, that something was not right with today. I can't put a finger on it."

The rest of the group stood and began heading back down the path. Bill took one last glance up the stairs before he turned to follow them.

CHAPTER

4

Back in the living chamber, several people were standing near the speaking platform and appeared to be waiting for Bill to get back. When he emerged from the tunnel, the people at the platform turned to watch. Soon, others saw him come in and moved to the platform to listen to what happened.

Bill went over to see his family first. Nancy took his hand as he walked over to brief the people about their test. When he got to the platform, he let go of Nancy and motioned for her to go back to her mother. She left his side, but kept looking back at him as she went.

Bill gave her a last wave before he got up on the platform. He signaled for the rest of his team to come up. After the team was together, Bill held up his hands to quiet the group. When things were quiet, Bill began, "As you probably know, we went outside to test the theory that these thermal blankets would not allow the aliens to see us." There was a slight murmur that went through the group, but he continued. "First, the bad news." Now a louder murmur started, but Bill talked a little louder, "Mike, I am sorry to say, your car does not exist anymore."

Everyone turned to Mike, and there were a couple of people near him who wished him their condolences. Mike lowered his head and waved a hand.

As Bill spoke again, everyone focused their attention back to him. "The good news is the experiment worked."

Now the group broke out into a cheer, and everyone started talking. Bill waited a little to continue. After the talk settled down, he explained. "Tom went out and laid in the parking lot for about an hour, and nothing happened. He then started Mike's car. Sorry, Mike." Mike shrugged as Bill went on, "When the car started, it took the aliens only a couple of seconds to show up. It checked the car out and destroyed it with its ray. After that, it circled the car twice and took off."

Bill stepped forward and continued, "This is telling us a couple of things. One, the blankets work. Two, because they got here so quickly that they must run patrols to check for more people. Third, because they didn't wait and only destroyed the car and left without landing. They were looking for people and didn't care about the car because nobody was in it."

Mike spoke up to say, "If they didn't care about my car, why did they destroy it?"

Bill shrugged his shoulders as he answered, "I don't know the answer to that. It could be as simple as eliminating a source of a false alarm."

There was a little talk about this. Bill let the discussion go on for a little while. Finally, he waved his hands to get everyone's attention. When he had everyone's attention, he laid out a plan. "Tomorrow, I want to send groups out. We should start with only one or two two-person groups to check out the houses and buildings right around us. If this works with no problems, we will expand our area with a couple more groups."

Someone for the group called out, "Why don't we just start sending people out now to get the things we need.?"

Bill slowly answered, "I don't want to take the chance that we might be wrong about the results of our experiment. We are making assumptions about what happened today. I don't feel completely comfortable with our conclusions. If I am wrong, we can still move ahead slowly. However, if I am right and send many people out, we can't take it back when they are all killed.'

This answer appeared to satisfy everyone, as most everyone was nodding in agreement.

Bill waited for a little and asked, "Okay, are there any more questions or ideas?"

While there was a lot of low talk, no one said anything out loud. Bill announced, "I would like to have a council meeting in about an hour. We can plan the details."

No one said anything to argue this decision, so Bill headed down off the platform and immediately headed for the men's room.

As soon as he went in, the smell hit him. He thought they were going to have to do something about this quickly. Mike was good at setting these things up. He could hand it over to Mike to handle.

When he came out of the men's room, he went straight to Mike. After explaining the situation, he and Mike came up with a plan to use the buckets from the food stores to bring water to flush the toilets. Now that he took care of that important job, Bill found his family and sat down to rest and think for a minute.

His wife and family came up and gathered around him. Nancy climbed into his lap while Judy and BJ sat on the floor. Finally, BJ asked, "Dad, when the aliens destroyed that car, was it like in the movies?"

Bill wasn't thinking that way. He had to think about it before he answered him. "Yeah, I guess it did. It was a solid line like the old ray guns in Star Trek."

BJ put his head down and said, "Wow." And asked, "What about the other ray that kills the people?"

Again, Bill wasn't thinking along these lines. However, as he thought about it, he realized it was different. Slowly he said, more thinking to himself than answering his son, "That one was different. It was a wide beam of light and a different color."

Nancy, who was listening, looked up at her father and asked, "What does that mean?"

Surprised, she realized the difference could mean something. Her father wasn't sure how to answer her. Bill glanced over at his wife as he said, "I'm not sure if it means anything. We simply don't know enough to answer those questions yet."

They all merely sat there in silence for a while. Soon, Bill saw the council members were already heading to the stairs. He lifted Nancy off his lap and got up. Looking at Judy, he said, "I'll be back when I can."

As she lifted Nancy onto her lap, she blew her husband a kiss before he turned to leave.

When Bill got to the stairs, there were only a few people there. He climbed up the stairs until he was sitting above the rest. Nobody said anything. They all sat in silence until the rest of the group showed up.

After a while, Bill took a quick headcount, and as best he could remember, the entire council was there. He began by asking, "Anyone have any ideas about what to do?"

Terry spoke up first. "I think we need to find a pharmacy first to get meds and medical supplies."

Bill looked over to Pam to ask, "Pam, do you know where the nearest pharmacy is?"

Pam looked around as she thought about it. Finally, she answered, "The closest place would be the Walmart just to the right when you leave, and I think there is a CVS in the little mall right next to Walmart."

"Great!" Bill exclaimed. "This gives us a place to start with that is very close. I think we should make you the official locator. I believe you are the only one in our group that has lived here, even for a short time. You know the town better than anyone else."

Pam started to say something, but after a moment, put her head down and said, "I'll do the best I can."

Bill asked her, "Is this a Super Walmart? Do they also sell food?"

Pam responded quickly. "Yes, they have food, and in the mall, with the CVS, and there is a grocery store near there." This time she spoke and with a little more authority, now that she realized she had an official position,

Bill simply said, "Excellent."

After a moment, he looked at the council. They appeared to agree with this idea, so he asked, "Does everyone agree that this is the place to start? Please raise your hands if you agree."

Slowly, everybody raised a hand. Now that the council decided on the first motion, Bill brought up the next part. "Who do we send?"

Now, this question started a round of discussion. Everyone had a different idea of who should go. The only thing that seemed to be a constant is that each of them thought they should be on the team. Bill let this go on for a while. When a few people got upset, he stood up to stop the discussion.

Slowly, he sat back down while everyone watched him. After a moment, he said, "I think we should send out two test groups for the first time out. We still don't know what our visitors can do."

Many in the group appeared to agree with this idea, so he continued, "In one group, I believe we send our good doctor, Terry, out. He is the only one that knows about medicines. He will also need someone to help watch his back." Again, more nods. Not hearing any idea from the rest, he said, "I will lead the second group to get supplies and food."

Still, no one said anything, but now he could see signs of the people we not as convinced as before. Bill continued to speak, "I think the remaining two to go out should be the people with the most experienced, our Marine and State Trooper."

Now the people argue about the last two choices. Most every one of them wanted to be in a team. When the arguing grew a little intense, Bill called for a stop and said, "This is another reason for the experienced ones to go out. We can't decide who else should be on these first two teams. If this comes off without a hitch, then we can send out more teams and spread out. The first time is going to be the most dangerous, and we will need people out there that know how to handle situations such as this."

The group was now thinking about Bill's reasoning, and many of the people appeared to agree again. Bill watched, and when he thought they settled it, he said, "Then we are all in agreement? Raise your hands if you agree with this plan."

All but two hands went up. So as not to single them out, Bill continued with, "This motion passes with a majority vote."

People got up to leave when Bill told them, "Wait a moment. We still have another issue to discuss."

They all looked around at each other and resumed their seats. When they were all settled, Bill brought up another problem. "I don't know if any of you have used the bathroom lately, but they are horrible. We need to assign jobs or duties to people to help. I have already assigned Terry as our community doctor. While not an actual doctor, he is the only one that I know of that had any kind of medical training. Second, it will also help to keep people's minds busy and help them get through this."

Mike now stood to say, "I have tried to assign things to people, but they either ignore me or say okay, but then don't do it."

Now a long debate started about what they could or should do. When it almost ended, most agreed that it was something that needed to be done. Bill suggested they meet tomorrow, after the trip outside, to discuss the supply run results and get ideas about the work problem.

Everyone agreed and got up to leave. Bill called his four people over and told them, "Today, we are on latrine detail. Those bathrooms must be taken care of now. I suggest we use the food containers to bring water back for flushing. Once the toilets are empty, we fill them one last time and leave them in there."

Tom now threw his two cents in. "The people aren't going to do what is needed on their own. They will have to be made to do it."

Bill merely shrugged his shoulders and replied, "I know, but this is a discussion for tomorrow."

With all of them in total agreement, they headed back to the living chamber.

Back in the chamber, Bill went over to his family and sat with them for a while. Nancy sat in his lap while BJ sat near his mother. It didn't take Nancy long to fall asleep. Gazing at her face, Bill had a little smile on his face. When he glanced up, he saw his wife staring at him with a smile of her own.

All too soon, Tom came over to ask quietly, "Sir, are we going to GI the latrines?"

Bill glanced down at Nance one more time and tried to lay her on the spot where she made her bed. It didn't work too well. She woke up and, in a panic, asked, "What's happening, Daddy?"

"Nothing, baby, you go back to sleep." He gently whispered to her.

Nancy sat on her bed a little while and suddenly jumped up to announce, "I'm going to go find Pam and play with her puppy."

As she went by her mother, Judy said, "Stay where I can see you."

Nancy said, back over her shoulder, "Okay, Mom."

As Bill and Tom walked towards the bathroom, Bill leaned over to say, "You don't have to call me Sir. I am retired, and they discharged you. Just try Bill from now on."

Tom gave a thumbs up and continued to walk to the bathroom.

As they walked, Bill waved to the others. Terry came running while Casey took a little longer. When they got to the men's room, they all could smell it outside. Unfortunately, down here, there was no ventilation, and the stench hung in the air.

Stopping short, Casey made a suggestion, "When you make the first trip out, I suggest you make an air freshener a top priority." She grabbed her nose as she cautiously moved closer.

"I'll say. Grab an entire case!" Terry agreed with her.

Bill picked up two food containers and headed to the lake they had been using. Tom grabbed the last of the buckets and followed.

On the way to the lake, Bill announced, "I want you to take Terry and hit the pharmacy in Walmart first. After, you'll go over to the drugstore. Casey and I will go into Walmart and start gathering supplies. I want to evaluate her tactical skill to see if she can lead a group later."

Tom nodded, but when Bill looked at him, Tom said, "Sure thing, Bill. That sounds good to me."

They continued onto the lake.

After getting the water, they each carried a bucket, and together they brought the third bucket back between them. When they got back to the bathrooms, both were out of breath. Bill thought it had been a long time since he last did this type of physical activity. He didn't realize how out of shape he was.

Casey and Terry had already started cleaning. They picked up the rooms and found trash cans to get rid of everything. Bill grabbed

Terry to take the rubbish cans outside to dump them. They took them upstairs and dumped them over the wall of junk for now. Bill realized he needed to put a stash of blankets up here for the instances they needed to step outside for things like this.

Once the garbage was out, Bill took Casey to help clean the ladies' room while Tom and Terry cleaned the men's room. While they were cleaning, Bill laid out his plan for him and her tomorrow. They would take the Walmart and see what supplies they would need right away. They would also stockpile others near the door for the next time they came there. Now he and she needed to think about what they would need right away.

Casey came up with the first thing, "Camp stoves and fuel."

Bill agreed, saying, "Good call. I'm getting a little tired of cold rations and the taste of the water."

Casey added, "Also, we'll need things to cook in and with."

Bill agreed as he continued to clean the stall. After a while, he thought about something else. "We need to find wagons and garden carts to carry things back to the cave."

"Agreed, but those will probably take time to assemble. I doubt they will already have assembled many. We will probably have to check the back rooms to find many of the things we will need. It means we'll need to bring lights."

Bill thought for a moment and said, "More lights might also make this place a little nicer. I believe they keep some of those fancy military-style lights upfront with a display of batteries. I say we stock up on those to use inside the store."

They both continued to clean the lady's room, and after a while, Bill stopped and said to Casey, "I think that will do it for the first supply run. Now about the food. I suggest we stay with cans and dry goods. By now, all the meat and produce will have gone bad." After thinking a moment, he added, "I think we should stop with the others to get masks to wear. There's no telling what might be still floating around in the air now."

After a couple of hours, the bathrooms were clean. However, the smell was going to take a lot longer to get rid of. They all met outside the bathrooms to talk together. After going over the plans, Bill brought up the last issue he felt they needed to deal with before going out tomorrow. "Now, I know this might be a touchy subject, but we will need to be armed out there. We have three firearms. All of them belong to Casey, but until we can find more, we are going to need to share them." Terry and Tom agreed.

Casey held her head down, so Bill went on, talking directly to her, "Casey, I know this goes against all your training. If it were me, I would feel the same way. But now you need to remember that I threw every bit of training, you and I have gotten, was thrown out the window when these things attacked. We are going to have to rewrite the entire book again. That starts with making do with what we have now."

Casey only nodded she understood. Finally, she said as she brought her head back up, "Okay, but I get my service gun. The rest of you can fight over the other two."

Bill laughed as he said, "Deal."

As the group broke up, Bill told Terry and Casey that it was their turn to get the water and leave one bucket in each room. Before he went to see his family, he said, "We'll meet first thing in the morning and get everything ready. I want to get this done as early as possible and make sure we are back well before dark."

The other three either mumbled an agreement or signaled with their hands that they understood. They all went off in different directions as Bill searched for Judy.

He found her talking to the other ladies, but she pardoned herself and went to meet him when she saw him. As they met, she threw her arms around his waist in a big hug. She took his arm and headed off down a path that led out of the living chamber. When she passed a lantern, she grabbed it so they could see.

Bill was thinking this was going to be one of those special moments. However, when Judy stopped, he could see, in the low light, the look on her face and lost all thoughts of getting lucky.

With a worried scowl on her face, she asked, "What are we going to do? What will happen to the children?"

Bill didn't know how to answer his wife. He figured a simple "I don't know" would not cut it with her. He reached out and pulled her close into a hug. After a while, he eased his hold on her, and when she put her head back, he gazed into her eyes to say, "We are going to survive."

Judy gave the hint of a smile and put her head back on his chest. She could hear his heart beating and thought it was a little fast. After a time, Bill released her and found a place to sit. He led her there, and they both sat on a rock. He held her hand in his lap as he thought about how to explain things while still giving her hope. "Honey, the first thing we are going to do is make a home. Right now, this is going to be this cave. Until we can find something better, this will have to do." He stopped, wishing he had brought a cup of water.

After a moment to gather his thoughts, he continued, "We can't find something that is going to work until we understand more about these aliens. We need to know what they want, what they intend to do to us and our civilization. We will need to fight them."

Judy never raised her head as he talked, but in a weak voice, she said, "I think it is fairly obvious what they intend to do with us."

Bill now slid sideways to face her. He grabbed both her hands as he said, "I disagree. I don't think it is obvious at all. I don't know for certain that the people I saw died. If they were going to kill all those people, why not use the same ray they used to destroy the bus? It was a different ray. When they destroyed the bus and car, those things remained. Melted and burning, but still they remained. The ray they used on the people made them disappear."

Now the analytical teacher within Judy was coming out. "Maybe this ray only works on biological things."

Bill had an answer for that. "That would explain the missing bodies and clothes made from plant or animal material. What about the man-made material? What about watches and glasses and gold rings? Those things would remain, but when I looked closer, I found nothing."

His wife had no answers.

Bill continued, "I'm not sure, but I think they were gathered up and taken somewhere. When they used the ray to take the people away, the craft left by going straight up. When they only used the destruction ray, it went back the way it came, back to its patrol area."

Now Judy was deep in thought. Bill waited a while, and when he could see she was as confused as he was, he added, "See, dear, things are not as simple and obvious as you might think. We have much to learn about these aliens before we can even think about what to do. We are on a new road. It will be long and winding, and we have only taken the first step."

When Judy's face relaxed and she glanced up at her husband he said, "Ask me this again when we get a mile or two down this road. I might have some ideas."

After a while longer, Bill stood and offered Judy his hand. She took it, and he pulled her up to kiss her. As they headed back to the group, he whispered, "Can I get some food? I'm starving."

Judy laughed a little, and when Bill joined her in the laugh, both of their spirits were riding high, and they had a good laugh before they rejoined the others again. Bill guessed he had quieted her concerns, for now.

The following day, Bill was up early. He set his phone to wake up to check things out before he met with his team. When he got to the stairs, he found Tom had the watch. When he reached the top of the stairs, he said nothing at first. They both scanned the sky and the ground. It was still too dark to make out much on the ground. However, the sun was going to break the horizon soon, and the sky was lightening. Everything was quiet. Bill asked Tom, "See anything last night?"

Tom reported, "Nothing in this direction, but last night I got out to check around behind us. I kept my blanket around me and stood out there for more than an hour. Back in that direction," Tom indicated to behind the opening where they were, "I saw what looked like two of those spacecrafts land. Later, I saw what I think was three taking off."

Bill thought about this for a moment and asked, "How far away were they?

Tom lowered his head to think before he answered. "It's hard to say. It could have been a mile or ten miles. The only thing I can think of is there might be a ground base there."

Bill walked down the stairs a little and sat down. Tom followed. When he decided, Bill said to Tom. "I agree. It sounds like a base of operations. I want to keep this between you and me for now. I don't want people to be distracted with other things like revenge until we get ourselves set up and have a better understanding of what is happening."

As Tom stood, and nodded to Bill, as he returned to his watch.

It wasn't long before Terry and Casey came up. Mike and a couple of other men were with them. Bill met them a little down from the top. When Tom joined the group, Bill gave the orders, "Tom, I want you to take Terry and use Casey's rifle to make your way out to the main road. Once you cross over, head to the west and go for the Walmart."

Terry had moved over with Tom, and they both showed their understanding.

Bill said to Casey. "You and I will follow, but stay on this side of the road. I'll take your carry pistol, and you'll have the service gun."

Reluctantly, Casey agreed.

After Tom and Terry took off, Bill said to Mike. "Mike, while we are out, see if you can get a couple of other men and try to find tables or counters to set up a food prep and serving area."

Mike said, "I got it. I see what you're trying to set up here."

Bill reminded him, "If you need to go out into the store area, remember to wear your blankets and keep your body heat hidden."

Mike laughed as he replied, "You can be certain of that."

Shortly, Casey called down from the top of the stairs, "They've made it to the road."

Bill didn't say anything. He rushed to the top and pulled out his little radio. Keying it, he called, "Tom, are you all clear?"

After a few seconds, Tom's voice came back. "Roger, we're just checking the situation before we cross. You can start your approach."

Bill didn't respond on the radio. He glanced at Casey and motioned with his head for them to move out. He was the first one over the wall, with Casey right behind him.

When they had cleared the store area, Casey was right beside him. Bill motioned for her to lean in as he whispered, "Keep your spacing. Stay about ten feet to the side. If you see something, yell at me and get down. We'll stay in place until it looks clear."

"Got it." Casey said, and as they moved out, she sarcastically added, "You Army guys sure do it a different way."

Bill said nothing. He headed for the road, but off to an angle, He did not want to follow in the same trail as Tom and Terry. When they got to the road, there was a small ditch that followed alongside it. He and Casey got down in the ditch and followed it.

They were lucky. The side Bill and Casey were on was mostly under cover of the trees. The other side, however, was out in the open.

When Bill and Casey got down to the Walmart area, they found several stores, shops, and restaurants. They burned some to the ground, while others showed no signs of being touched. While they waited for Tom and Terry. Bill set up in a donut shop and tried to understand the why of everything. He studied the situation. Some shops were burned while other shops were left untouched. He found the same pattern in the cars in the lot. Many were destroyed, while others were only burned, and yet more were left alone. The only thing that was the same was, again, no bodies.

After a short time, Casey spotted the other two making their way through the parking lot towards Walmart. Bill keyed up his radio and called, "Tom, we have you in sight. We'll meet you at the front of the store."

Tom had a simple. "Copy." For a reply.

The four of them met at the corner of the Walmart building. Bill signaled for everyone to follow him. He went in through the garden area and found the side door. Before going in, he took a few moments to study the inside through the doors. Everything appeared to be normal, except being dark and no people.

Once inside, they found carts all around the store. Some were full of items, while others had very little. They found women's handbags in the baby seat or inside the cart. When they checked them, there was money, identification, and other things. It appeared nothing else was taken.

When they made their way to the front of the store, they found the stand with flashlights and batteries. After getting the batteries installed, they each had their own flashlight and began scanning the store.

Bill checked the checkout line. He found the cash register open with a small amount of cash either spread out on the belt like it was simply dropped there or on the floor. He even found one with the debit card still in the machine. When he checked the name, it was the same name on the driver's license in the bag in the cart.

After the initial shock of what they found, they got to work. Tom and Terry headed over to the pharmacy area while Bill and Casey went to the garden area to find wagons. Casey was wrong. There was one already put together and two more in boxes on the shelf. They grabbed a couple of shopping carts and took the wagons to the tool section to pick up what they needed to put them together.

In the store's front, where there was a lot of light, Bill and Casey quickly assembled the wagons. They split up. While Bill went to the outdoor section to find camp stoves, Casey headed for the food. They planned to fill up carts and have them staged near the front of the store so they could make quick trips to get the things they needed.

Meanwhile, Tom and Terry found the pharmacy area and started loading up carts with their loot. They quickly broke into the back room, and while Terry went through the medicines, Tom started grabbing personal things. They needed such items as toothbrushes and toothpaste, soap and shampoo, and, most importantly, deodorant.

Bill found backpacks in the camping area. He quickly took those upfront to Terry to load all the meds in. When he returned, he found four camp stoves and several cans of fuel and several dozen little propane bottles. He grabbed the stoves, fuel, and propane and put them in his cart. As he was ready to push them out to the front, he found a good stash of lanterns. Both gas and battery. He would have to make a second trip for them.

Casey went straight for the can foods. She started raking piles of cans into her cart. When Bill got to the staging area with his first cart, he found two baskets already full of canned goods.

Tom and Terry finished with their shopping, but before they headed off to the CVS, Tom brought a pack of masks to Bill and Casey. The smell wasn't too bad yet, but it was growing, along with who knows what else in the air.

After a couple of hours, Bill got Casey, and they found food they could eat. The bread row was still good, and most of the cheese was good. They didn't dare try any of the meat, however, they found cans of the little hot dogs and made sandwiches.

As they were finishing their lunch, they heard a gunshot. Immediately, instinct kicked in, and they both jumped up and ran to the front of the store. The doors were still open from when Tom and Terry left. After a quick check of the area to make sure it was clear, they made a quick dash to the CVS. Again, the door was open.

Bill and Casey took up positions on each side of the door. Bill signaled for them to go in, to the opposite side, and take up positions there. Once they were inside, they made their way slowly into the store. They heard sounds from the back where the pharmacy counter was and headed that way. When they got close, they found the body of a large dead dog.

Bill waited until he saw Tom come back to the front counter with an armload of medicines. Slowly, Bill stood where Tom saw him. It scared the shit out of him, and he dropped all the medication he was carrying. After catching his breath, Tom glanced down at the dog and back at Bill. With a sheepish face, he said, "Sorry, Sir. I probably should have called you on the radio. I didn't think about it."

Bill put his gun away and walked up to the counter. Staring right at Tom, he asked, "What happened?"

Terry joined them at the counter, and Tom started his story. "We made it into the store, and just like Walmart, it was empty. We came right back to the pharmacy area and got the things Terry said we needed. When I brought out a load, there was that dog up the aisle. It charged, so I dropped everything and killed it."

When Bill said nothing, Terry added, "We didn't think it was going to be friendly."

Bill almost choked on a laugh. It wasn't really that funny, but the way he said it hit him right after the tense situation they expected to find.

Everyone laughed, but it didn't last too long. Bill got serious, and the others followed. "Alright, new rule." He said, "When you enter a store through an open door, close the door behind you and clear the store before you shop."

Tom again made a sheepish face and replied, "Got it, loud and clear."

As Bill went to leave, he added over his shoulder, "And make better use of the radios. That's what we have them for."

As Bill continued to walk to the front of the store, he heard, "You got it." From the two voices in the back of the store.

Bill and Casey went back to Walmart and continued with their shopping until it was late in the afternoon. Tom and Terry returned with the stuff they got from CVS and helped with the shopping. Before they left, they arranged the carts in the order of what they thought they would need for each trip. They loaded up the little wagons, and with all of them carrying a full backpack, they headed back.

It took several hours to get back. First, it was very cumbersome trying to carry the backpack, pull the wagon, and keep the blanket over them. They even spotted one of the alien craft nearby and got down and froze. After it passed, they stayed frozen for about half an hour. When the craft never came back, they slowly got up and made it the rest of the way home.

Once back inside the cave, Bill immediately headed for the talking platform, with his crew following him. The entire population of the cave began cheering as soon as they came into sight. Everyone also moved toward the platform.

Bill waited until everyone had gathered and quieted down before he spoke. "We had a lot of success on this trip."

Again, there was an enormous round of cheers. Bill had to wait to continue as he showed the fully loaded wagons. "We gathered enough food and cookware to set up a nice little kitchen area. No more cold dinners." Another round of cheers. When it was quiet, Bill called Terry to the front with him. "Our Doctor, Terry, hit it big with the load of medicine and supplies he brought back."

More cheering, but this time, it wasn't as strong. Bill continued, as if nothing had changed. "We also found a few air mattresses, and we'll figure out a way to decide who gets the first load."

This time, there was a little stir as people started talking about this announcement. He didn't wait to continue. "We also brought back other supplies we thought would be good to have. We set up carts at the front of the store to make quick trips to bring in more food and supplies."

This time, Bill waited for it to quiet down. "Now, we know we can go out, if we are careful!" He put a lot of emphasis on the last part. Continuing, he added, "Tomorrow, we will send out a couple more teams in different directions. However, the news is not all good."

Bill stood there until he was sure he had everyone's attention. Slowly he told them, "We had a run-in with a dog. This dog was a house pet that had turned vicious. When it attacked, we had to kill it. So, whoever goes out will do so at your own risk. Also, you must remember there are aliens you'll need to deal with. We know what happens if they see you."

Now everyone was quiet as they thought about that last part. Bill added, "We'll set up the supply point in a little while, and people can come by to see if they need anything. Terry is going to set up a medical area, and he'll let you know when he is ready to see new patients." Before he left the speaking platform, Bill also shouted, "Could I see Susan up here?"

By the time Bill got down to the main floor, Susan was there waiting for him. Before he could say anything, Susan spoke up to say, "Thank you so much for everything you're doing for us. I don't think we would have made it past the first day if you hadn't stepped up to take control."

Bill shyly said, "Thank you. It is just something the Army drilled into me." He saw a couple of other ladies who appeared to be waiting for Susan. He asked, "Are these your friends you were traveling with?"

Susan waved to the ladies. When they waved back, she turned back to Bill. He asked, "You said you worked as a cook in a school?" When Susan nodded, Bill continued, "Did these ladies work with you?"

Susan simply said, "Yes."

"Great," Bill said. "I would like you three to run the food prep area. We have four camp stoves, and when we go out again, you can give us lists of other things you think you'll need. I figure setting up a cafeteria type of setup. People can file by and fill up their plates. However, you are the expert, so you can set it up any way you think best."

"Can I go ask them if they want to do this?" Susan asked.

"Certainly. I'll be over with my family when you decide."

As Susan went over to her friends and Bill headed back to his family area.

Before he reached his family, Susan ran up to say, "They all agreed. We also need to help."

Bill was happy with the news from her. He scanned the area to find Mike, and when he did, he said, "That is great. Now you need to see Mike, over there," he said as he pointed. "He will set up the area the way you want it."

Susan clasped her hand under her chin with a big grin on her face and ran to go find Mike. Bill thought as he watched her that Tom might not be right about these people. It appeared to him the people needed something to do that showed they have value for the group.

When he found his family, Bill kissed and hugged everyone as his wife gave him a plate of cold food to eat. He was so hungry he didn't wait to see if there would be hot food tonight. He simply took the food from Judy and started eating.

CHAPTER

5

Over the next couple of weeks, the little community was well supplied and ready to widen their search area. Bill was up early, as usual. After checking the watch on the stairs, he went to the men's room to wash up. The smell was still there, but this time it was better. He figured there was nothing they could do about it. Even if there was ventilation, there was no electricity to make it work.

When Bill came out of the men's room, there was a much more pleasant smell to greet him. Surveying the group, he found Susan and her two helpers in the brand new kitchen area, cooking up breakfast for everyone. When he walked up to the table, they were using it as a counter; he found a large stack of paper plates, napkins, and plastic utensils. It almost looked like a regular lunch counter.

When Susan turned and saw him, she smiled and came over to the counter. After checking up and down the length of the counter, she asked, "Well, what do you think?"

Bill took in the entire setup. Smiling, he replied, "You ladies have done a fantastic job. Everything looks and smells great."

Susan told him, "Grab a plate and stuff, and we'll serve you up breakfast. We got scrambled powdered eggs, some sausage, and we even have real coffee. I don't know how the coffee is going to taste, though. We had to make it with the same awful drinking water."

Bill figured any coffee was better than no coffee. He grabbed a plate and the other things and moved down the line. One lady scooped up eggs and put it on his plate. The next lady put a piece of sausage on the plate, and Susan handed him a styrofoam cup of coffee. As she did, she told him, "There is sugar and powder creamer over on the little table."

Bill moved over to the little table set up just as she said. He and glanced back at Susan, who had a very proud face, and he asked, "Where did you get all this stuff?"

She indicated the entire row and said, "You guys brought back the plates and stuff. We emptied several packs of powder eggs from the food packs. One of you brought back this sausage and bacon meat packs, that doesn't need to be refrigerated. We figured today we'll do sausage, and tomorrow we'll have bacon."

Bill shook his head, and as the other two ladies came up, he laughed as he said, "I guess I sure picked the right group of people to run the kitchen. All of you are to be commended for what you have put together for us."

He took a sip of coffee. He may have been wrong about thinking this would be better than no coffee, but he smiled and lifted his cup to the ladies. When he left, he went over to his family to sit and eat. The food was great, but needed salt and pepper. He got up and went to the little table, and sure enough, there were a couple of salt and pepper shakers there.

Returning to his spot, he finished his breakfast. It was the best meal he had had in a couple of days. He made a note to find out who found the meat and thank them. Now he needed to plan today's ventures into the town. First, he needed to figure out what they still needed. Everything was all set for meds. The food was now okay, and they had an excellent source that was close. Weapons and ammunition were low. Bill was unsure if there were any gun shops in the area. Walmart stopped carrying such things. Maybe they have some archery equipment. This would have to be on everyone's list. Warmer clothes and blankets or sleeping bags should be high on the list. Bill planned to take Pam and maybe someone else and head back to Walmart. They still needed to get more personal things, like lady's needs and such.

He now had some ideas. However, the others stirred, so his planning time was over. He stood and began directing people to the kitchen for breakfast. When he ran into Mike, he pulled him aside to thank him and told him what a great job he had done setting this all up. Mike was still a little sleepy, but when Bill thanked him, he woke right up, and his chest came out. Mike was a good man, and Bill was glad he had challenged him for leadership. Otherwise, they might never have met, or at least taken longer to meet.

He found his little team eating together. He joined them, and as he finished the coffee, he laid out his plans so far. It was Casey who came up with another thing.

Slowly saying, as she held a cup of coffee with both hands and gazing into it like she could read a fortune or something, "What about people? I mean, we can't be the only survivors. What do we do if we find others out there?"

Casey had made a good point. Bill hadn't even considered the possibility of others being still alive. He sat there staring at her as he thought. Finally, he said to the group, "Time for another short council meeting."

Bill stood and headed to find Mike. He found him with a small group. As he approached the group, they all stopped talking and looked up at him.

"Mike," Bill called as he walked up.

Mike put down his cup and came away from his group. After bumping into someone and spilling that man's coffee, he made it to Bill. "What's up?" he asked.

"Mike, I was talking with my team, and we discovered a little situation we might run into out in the new world. We need to have a little council meeting before we go out today."

"I'll grab everyone. What time do you want to meet?" Mike responded.

"Let's meet in an hour at the usual place."

"Got it. That will let people finish eating and get ready. See you then," Bill said and went back to get his cup of coffee.

As Bill returned to his group, he saw Mike already searching for the council members. He knew Mike would get it done. As he sat down, he asked, "Anyone else have any ideas?"

Tom spoke up this time. "I suggest we organize our search of the town for now. We send groups on the four cardinal headings and see what we can find. When you reach a spot by noon, you turn right, go a couple of blocks, and head back."

As Tom was talking, Bill listened and nodded his agreement to the idea. When Tom finished, Bill asked, "What do the rest of you think?"

Casey nodded as she said, "Sound like a good plan. We can cover the town without wasting time searching places someone else has already searched."

Terry still had food in his mouth, so he merely nodded his agreement with Tom as he pointed to him.

Bill stood up to say, "Okay, we'll run with that for now and see how it works. We'll have a short meeting this morning before we go out to discuss what Casey brought up. I'll see you guys in about forty-five minutes."

No one responded to him as Bill headed towards his family. Running this group was taking way too much time away from his family. He needed to do more things with them. This issue would need to be a high-priority item on his long list of things to do.

After sitting with his wife and kids and discussing the events, Bill thought the children had a very good handle on what was happening. He thought Nancy understood the situation, but didn't fully comprehend all that it meant. BJ, on the other hand, was up to date with all the happening and asking the right questions which showed he understood all this meant. He was eager to join a group and go out on patrols.

Bill would have to think about this and certainly get his wife's approval, but he will monitor his son and watch his development.

After more family chatting, Bill left his family and headed for the usual council meeting place. A few had already gathered. There was the usual small talk while they waited for the rest of the council to show up.

When everyone was there, Bill stood up to signify the meeting was starting. The talking almost immediately stopped. He could see in nearly all the faces a much fresher outlook. They appeared to be more confident in what they were doing, and Bill thought he could see hope in their eyes. When he took his usual place, he started talking. "Good morning to all of you. I hope you had an excellent breakfast."

As he paused, the entire group made comments, all positive, about the surprise meal they had. They chatted among themselves, but Bill wanted to continue with the reason he called this meeting. He held up both hands, and everyone stopped talking and watched him.

Bill immediately brought up the subject they had gathered to discuss. "While talking with my team this morning, an issue came up. I felt it needs to be addressed by the council." He didn't pause this time and went right at it. "Casey brought up the subject of others. We can't be the only ones to survive. The question is, what do we do if we find others that are out there and hiding, just like us?"

There was immediate silence. A lot of heads went down as if thinking about it. The other people were glancing around at those who appeared to be thinking.

It was Mr. Taylor who spoke first. "Yes, this is an important issue. So far, we have been very fortunate with the group we have. If we let anyone join our group, we might ask for a great deal of trouble."

Before Jim could sit back down, Linda, the business manager, jumped right in. "Of course we need to help everyone we can. What's happing is, as the scientist would say, an extinction-level event. We must do everything we can to protect our species. We either help supply them, or better yet, bring them into our group."

As the discussion now broke down into little groups and pairs, Bill thought about it. Right off the bat, the only two views were at the opposite end of the extreme actions. Either we bring them in like family or keep them out and possibly doom humanity to extension.

Bill let the talk go on for a while before raising his hands to bring order back to the meeting. When it was all quiet, he stood up and took a step down as he considered the council. Slowly, he spoke. "I can see there are many views on this issue. I would suggest we end the discussion for now. During the day, we talk with those who put each of us on the council and with each other to see if there is a middle ground, we can all agree on."

All the members showed they agreed. Mike announced, "I would like to second this."

It surprised Bill that Mike knew about the rules of a meeting and jumped right in. It would appear Mike is taking his role in this community seriously. Bill said, "All in favor of this course, raise your hands."

Everyone's hand went up. As Bill looked at each member, he nodded to them and announced, "It is decided. We will meet back in a day or so and discuss this matter in greater detail. In the meantime, see how everyone else feels. Also, try to come up with a compromise somewhere in the middle that would work."

Slowly the council broke up, and those that were not interested in going out left. A couple of people remained with Bill and his team. Quickly, Bill assigned the teams. He gave them a list of things they needed to search for now and to take notes about where other stashes of things they might need in the future were.

Each group decided in what direction they were going to head. Bill announced he would take Pam and head east to the Walmart to see what else they could find. However, before leaving, he and Pam went back to the main area to find one other person.

Pam went off to find another person to join them while Bill checked in with his family. As he told Judy of his plans, BJ overheard him say they were getting one more person to go with him.

BJ jumped up and shouted, "Dad, can I go with you?"

Bill glared at him and back at Judy. The expression on her face said no. He slowly took him by the shoulders. Looking him straight in the face, he said, "I'm sorry, but not this time. Before you go with me, I will need to teach you some things about how we work outside now. When I come back today, you and I will start your training. You'll need to learn how we move and what our signals are, and many other things."

This reasoning appeared to satisfy BJ, for now. However, Judy still did not appear to be happy with the idea. Luckily for Bill, Pam came back with someone, and he used that as an excuse to get away without further discussion of the matter.

As the three of them walked to the stairs, Pam introduced the new person as Ahmed. Bill offered his hand, and there was a quick handshake as they reached the bottom of the stairs.

Bill took a couple of steps up and to where he normally sat. Pam and Ahmed also sat on the steps. Checking Ahmed, Bill asked, "Where are you from?"

Ahmed first glanced to Pam and back to Bill before answering. "I am here in America on a work visa from the United Arab Emirates. I completed my work, so my wife and I are traveling to see this wonderful country before we must go home. We only started our travels, and now I don't think we will return home."

Bill nodded to Ahmed and added, "Yes, I think it will not be possible for any of us to go home now."

They all took a moment to think about this revelation. Bill continued to question the new man. "What experience do you have in situations, and I hate to say it this way, but in situations like this?"

Ahmed answered. "In my work as a communication's technical adviser, I traveled around the world. I spent much of the time in my area of the world. You know the Middle East is a very war-torn area. I have learned to hide and evade when necessary. If you don't learn these skills early, you do not live very long."

Bill only studied Ahmed for a moment and quickly stood up and again offering his hand; he said, "Sounds good enough to me. We will go slowly. You watch what we do, and if anyone sees something, you sound off and quickly hide under the thermal blanket and don't move. I will give the all-clear. Sometimes it can take more than an hour, so relax and stay calm."

Heading up the stairs, Bill led the way to the top, where they took cover while taking the time to check the skies for any of the alien crafts. He slowly headed out and around the corner to head towards Walmart. Bill glanced back to see Pam following and Ahmed bringing up the tail. Pam showed Ahmed where he should go and what to do. It was like they had done this before.

They made their way to Walmart with no trouble. It wasn't long before they gathered a lot of things people needed. One area they wiped out was the deodorant aisle. It had become almost a regular daily laugh about how they all smelled terrible. Even with the bathroom wash-ups, it was not enough. Everyone certainly needed deodorant. Bill felt it would be a good thing to help lighten up everyone's mood.

After about an hour, Bill got a call on his radio. It was Casey calling. "Bill. You copy?"

Pulling the radio from his pack, Bill replied, "I copy, loud and clear."

In a calm, clear voice, Casey said, "I need you to come to me. We have a situation."

Considering at his two companions, who were also listening, Bill asked, "What kind of situation?"

It took a little while before she answered, but still calm, Casey replied, "We'll discuss it when you get here. Nothing dangerous. I need your guidance."

It was undoubtedly a dodge to his question. Now he was extremely curious about this situation that she did not want to discuss over the radio.

He keyed up his radio and simply said, "Copy. On our way. Where are you?"

"We are on 211, the main drag, about a mile into town. Just over the river, but before the train."

Pointing at Pam, Bill asked, "You know where she is?"

Pam nodded, so Bill replied, "Copy. We know where you're at. We'll be there as soon as we can."

He waited a moment, but since there was no response from Casey, Bill said, "Let's move out and go see what's up."

When they got to the edge of the parking lot, Bill stopped, and when the others got to him, he said to Pam, "You know the area, so you take the lead."

Pam didn't move. A look of fear came over her face, and Bill saw it. He whispered to her, "Pam, you know the area better than any of us. You have been out on these patrols several times over the last couple of weeks. You know what you are doing. Take it slow and keep a good watch." Glancing at Ahmed, he added, "We'll all keep a good watch."

Ahmed only nodded back to him.

She still hadn't moved, so Bill motioned with his hands for her to move out.

Pam took her time and carefully scanned the area as they advanced. She moved up to the edge of the road, and like Bill had taught her, she checked both ways and made a complete circle of the sky before she crossed. When she got to the other side, she got down on the ground and covered with her blanket.

Bill watched Ahmed and motioned for him to move up. When he was close, Bill told him, "Do exactly as she did. Clear the road and skies before you cross. Cross quickly and find a spot not too close to her and get down and cover. Any question."

Ahmed shook his head and moved. Bill watched as Ahmed crossed and could see that he had done this before.

Now it was Bill's turn, but before he could cross, Pam called out, "Cover!"

Bill immediately dropped. In one smooth move, he brought his blanket up over his head to cover himself. He laid there waiting for the all-clear. This time, he would have to rely on Pam to give the all-clear because he hadn't seen the problem.

- In about ten minutes, Pam gave the all-clear, and Bill finished his crossing. He got down a few feet from her and asked, "What did you see?"

"One of those crafts. It was low over the trees, near the caves. It didn't stop or even slow down. As soon as it was out of sight, I figured it was clear."

Bill double check the area she had pointed to, and after a moment to think, he told her, "Good job. We'll need to keep an eye in that direction more."

Pam continued to lie there and Bill finally had to tell her, "Okay, let's continue."

This time, they had no more problems and fairly quickly made it to the river in the middle of the town.

Bill moved up to take the lead. After he saw the situation, he decided the bridge wasn't too long, and there were a couple of cars stopped along the side of the road they could use for cover. He motioned for the other two to come up. He quickly explained, "We're going to do this just like the road crossings. We'll break it into two parts. I'll go halfway. Once I'm undercover, each of you will come up near me. We'll do this again to finish crossing. Questions?"

Both his teammates shook their heads. Bill quickly took off and made his way to the center of the bridge. Pam and Ahmed, both followed him, and they each repeated the move to finish the crossing.

They took cover in a little building on the other end of the bridge. As Bill was taking out his radio, Casey called, "Nice textbook crossing. We are in the church at the top of the hill, on the other side of the road."

Bill had to laugh at Casey's comment and replied, "Copy. See you in a few."

Checking his team, he again gave the sign to move out. They crossed the road and made their way up to the church. Inside, Bill found Casey waiting for him. She motioned for them to follow, and they went upstairs to where the rest of her team was.

Bill immediately saw her team spread out, so each had a window. They were scanning the town with binoculars. "What's up, and why all the secrecy on the radio?"

"Well, we had one of those situations we talked about this morning, and I wasn't sure what to do about it."

It took Bill a moment to realize what she was talking about. Quickly it hit him, and he almost shouted, "You mean you saw others?"

Casey nodded and moved toward one window. She pointed down the road. "You see that building with the flag on the other side of the tracks?"

Bill took out his binoculars to see better. "Yeah, I see it. What is it?"

"Best guess is it is a police station or a fire station."

Bill glanced again, but from this angle, he couldn't decide either. "What about it?"

"Shortly after we got here, one of my guys spotted two people going into that building. He guessed from the looks of them; they were both kids."

Pam now spoke, "Kids! What are kids doing out here by themselves?"

Bill sat on the floor with his back to the wall. Scanning the room, he said, "First off, we don't know for sure they are kids. Second, we had better assume they are not alone and there or others." He asked Casey. "Why didn't you say so over the radio?"

"Not knowing what to do yet, I didn't want the others in the cave to get all excited about our new find until I checked with you."

Thinking about her reasoning, Bill nodded his agreement with her decision. He sat there for a while, thinking. Finally, he got on his radio and called the other two teams. "Tom and Terry, if you copy, check in."

There was no word from Tom. His group had gone north and may be out of range. Terry, however, checked in, "Terry here, we copy."

They could all hear his signal was strong. Bill asked, "Where are you?"

Terry came right back. "We went south. Not much there but farmland and the high school. When we heard Casey's call, we moved west and crossed the tracks south of town. We made our way back. We are now in a graveyard. I believe we are past the tracks on the same road."

Bill thought about the whole situation for a while. He didn't know if they should make contact or not. Considering Casey and Pam, who were both council members and the only other ones from the council, he asked, "Working as part of the council, what do you think?"

Pam jumped right in. "We go get them. If they are kids, they shouldn't be let out here alone."

Casey nodded. "Yes, I agree, but we need to be careful. We do not know who is there and what weapons they might have."

Bill also nodded to both of them. "We need to get word to Terry without using the radio. I also agree with Casey's reasoning to keep this off the air until we know more."

Casey volunteered. "I can make my way around to him and let him know what to do. What do you want him to do?"

Bill got up and stared out the window for a moment. Sitting down, he laid out his plan. "Okay, I'll stay here with this group. Casey, you swing around and contact Terry. When you get with him, signal me, and we'll move. We'll make our way up the street on this side. You and Terry take the other side of the street and move back down this way.

We'll get as close as we can without being seen. Once we are in position, I'll take a small group, one or two, and make our way in."

Casey asked, with a little concern, "Do you think a couple of people will be enough? What if there is a problem?"

He replied, "The problem is exactly why I'm taking a small group. If there are a bunch of well-armed people in there, I don't want to risk the entire group. If there is no problem, I don't want to scare the people there to death with a large group. Especially if they are children."

Casey realized Bill was right. She simply nodded to him as she left.

Before she got out of the room, Bill added, "I'll let Terry know you're coming. I wouldn't want anyone to take a shot at you." He put on a big grin for her.

Sarcastically smiling back, Casey was out the door.

Bill told the rest of the people there, "Everyone, keep a sharp eye out for any movement. If you see anything, sing out, even if it's Casey. I want to keep track of her."

It took almost an hour for Casey to get around to Terry. During that time, only one person saw her and only when she crossed the road. She radioed in that they were ready at their end.

Bill gathered up his group and made their way up the street. When he made his way around behind the buildings, he found a brick building close to the tracks that gave a good view of the building with the flag. The building he was in was the police station, and the building with the flag was the fire station. He had a good, clear view of the fire station. All the doors were closed, and everything appeared to be deserted.

Once he had his team set, Bill called Terry. It was Casey that answered and told him they were right behind the fire station. There was a little hill, and she didn't see any doors on this side or the far end.

Bill took Ahmed with him. While they were at the police station, they found weapons. There was a shotgun and two pistols. He gave the shotgun to Ahmed, and he kept one pistol. He handed the rifle he had to Pam. The way she handled it, Bill made a note to himself to train everyone that goes out about guns.

Bill and Ahmed made their way behind another building to the corner next to the tracks. There was a little park with a sharp hill they could hide behind. Bill used the binoculars to scan the front of the fire station. There were two glass doors and a large glass window at this end. The doors to the vehicle bays were all closed. It appeared the only way inside was through the two front doors.

The only way to get there was out in the open, in about every direction. There was a slight slope to the ground so they might get close by using a belly crawl. Going over the maneuver with Ahmed first, Bill felt confident they could make it if no one was watching.

The two of them spread out a little and crawled across the tracks and up to the fire station. It took a while, and both were tired by the time they got there. Now they could see through the windows. There was nobody in sight. Bill tried the front door. This one being locked; he checked the other door. This one opened and the two of them slowly moved inside.

After waiting for their eyes to adjust to the darkness, Bill and Ahmed slowly move further into the building. There was enough light coming in through the windows that they could now see. Bill moved to the back of the building and signaled for Ahmed to move around the front.

As Bill moved along the back, he heard voices. There appeared to be only a couple of people, and as he got closer, he could tell at least one of them was a child's voice. A girl's voice, he thought. Ahmed made his way around and started coming in Bill's direction. Bill signaled to be quiet and pointed to a closed door.

They both listened for a while. There appeared to be two children. One boy and one girl. The boy was obviously in charge and was probably older. The two children were talking to someone else. Although he could tell someone was there, Bill couldn't make out who it was or what they said. However, from the talk, Bill understood the third person might be hurt.

Slowly, Bill tried the door. Not being locked, he pushed it open. It had moved only a couple of inches when it made a squeak. Suddenly, Bill heard the distinct sound of a rifle being cocked. He backed out before, whoever it was, fired the shot. It harmlessly hit high on the wall.

Bill shouted out, "Hold your fire! We mean you no harm. We are looking for supplies and anyone else that might have survived."

Now Bill heard another voice. It sounded like an older woman. "Don't come in. We are well armed." After a brief pause, the woman added, "Who are you?"

Okay, Bill thought. They want to talk. He sat against the wall and replied, "My name is Bill. We are also well-armed, but we don't want to end up in a shootout. I am the leader of a small group of people who, like yourselves, have survived this attack."

"What do you mean, attack?" The woman asked back in a shocked voice.

Bill hadn't counted on this. Because they had figured it out, he thought everyone would know by now. How do you tell someone aliens destroyed the world?

He wasn't sure what to do. Softly, he asked, "What do you know?"

She replied, "Nothing. I laid down to take a nap a couple of weeks ago, and when I woke up, everyone was gone."

It surprised Bill that she knew absolutely nothing about the attack and that they have been able to survive. He hung his head down a moment while he figured out what to say.

After a moment, he quietly asked, "What's your name?"

There came a calmer reply now. "Danny."

"Danny, I am here with another man, Ahmed. There are others outside that are waiting to hear from me. I am going to let them know everything is good and that we are talking. I won't bring them in until you say it is Okay. Is that alright with you?"

It took a little while for her to answer, and Bill could hear whispered discussion about it, but Danny finally said, "That is fine. I don't want anyone to get hurt, either."

Bill pulled out his radio and called Terry. Again, it was Casey that answered.

"What happened? We heard a shot and didn't hear from you. We were getting ready to rush the place."

Bill quickly responded, "Stay put. We are alright. There was a little misunderstanding. But we are talking now. I will let you know what happens. For now, just search around the area and see if you can find anything useful."

Casey replied in a cautious voice, "If you're sure you're alright, okay. Keep in touch."

Bill keyed up and replied, "Copy."

Bill called out to Danny, "Everything is good now. My group outside is going to check around the area to see what we can use."

Danny responded. "I don't think you'll find much. We've cleaned out the area pretty good."

Bill realized she didn't even hear her mistake. He slowly asked, "We?"

A muffled, "Shit!" was her only response.

Bill tried to reassure her that everything was alright, "Yes, we know you have at least two children with you. I have a wife and two children of my own, back where we are hiding."

There was a long pause before Danny responded, "I don't want any trouble. We want to be left alone."

Bill now talked gently to her, "I know you don't want trouble, and neither do we. The problem is, I don't think you understand what is happening. This situation is not a simple thing that is going to go away. You and your children have a very low chance of surviving by yourself."

There was no reply for Danny this time. Bill tried pushing her a little. "It is very difficult for us to talk through this door. Would you mind if I came in and sat next to the door? I will come in unarmed, and you can search me if you like. I need you to believe we at not the danger here."

There was a long wait while Bill heard a discussion between Danny and her children. He could not make out what they were saying, but it sounded like the kids were okay with the idea.

Finally, Danny responded, "You have another person with you?"

"Yes."

"Send him away, and you can come in. Be very slow when you do. I'll have the rifle on you at all times."

Bill went to Ahmed and handed him the pistol. As he told him to leave, Bill heard the squeak of the door as Ahmed quickly went out the same way they came in. Before Bill could turn back to Danny, he heard it close again.

Knocking on the door, Bill asked, "May I come in now?"

Danny answered, "Slowly and carefully. If you make any sudden moves, I will shoot you."

Bill didn't know who fired the first shot, but he believed Danny was not very good with the rifle. However, she might get lucky, so he slowly opened the door enough to see in. There were clothes and food all around. They had been busy cleaning out the neighborhood. He didn't see anyone, so he stepped through the door. Again, he heard the rifle cock, but this time there was no shot fired. Raising his hands, he announced, "I am unarmed. You can check me if you like."

Danny's voice came from around the corner. She flatly said, "Lay on your belly with your face right on the floor. Move slowly."

Bill got down on the floor and put his nose right on the floor. He heard the feet scuffing and could see a small shoe next to his head. He felt the hands as they checked his body from head to toe. The person moved away, and Danny spoke again. "Okay, you're clean. Now I want you to get on your hands and knees and move over to the wall and sit."

Bill did as she told him. When he finally turned to sit, he saw a woman he guessed was in her late twenties, maybe early thirties. He saw two children hiding behind her. He thought the boy might be about the same age as BJ and the girl seemed to be a little older than Nancy.

Bill and Danny sat there, staring at each other for a little. Bill finally spoke and said, "My name is Bill Jenson. I live here in Virginia, near DC. My wife and family came here to go through the caves and were down inside when all this happened."

The boy shouted out, "You saw what happened?"

Danny quickly turned and shushed the boy. Turning back to Bill, she asked, "Do you know what is going on? We have seen no one in a couple of weeks."

Before he could answer, Danny shifted her body a little. He could see she was in quite a bit of pain. "Are you alright?" he asked.

The little girl sadly said, "She fell yesterday, and we think her leg is broken."

Bill could see the bottom of her leg, all wrapped up down to her toes. He could tell it was probably the work of the kids. Pointing to her leg, Bill told her, "I have a Navy medic on my team outside. He's not a doctor, but he has treated people in combat in the Middle East. I could call him in here to check that, if you like."

Suddenly, there was a scared expression in Danny's eyes. "Why do you have a military medic?"

Bill understood her concern. "He was on shore leave and came to check out the caves as well. I can tell you we have about thirty people in my group. We were all taking the tour of the cave and were underground when everything happened. That saved us."

Danny was a little relieved at his explanation. She glanced at her kids and back at Bill. Slowly she said, "You can call your man in. The same rules apply to him you agreed to."

"Fair enough." Bill said and reached for the radio.

Danny pulled the rifle up to her shoulder and pointed it at him.

Bill froze. Using only his fingers, he slowly pulled the radio out of his shirt pocket and showed it to her.

She carefully lowed the rifle and nodded to Bill.

He quickly keyed up the radio and called Terry. Again, Casey answered the call. "Terry's busy. What's up?"

Bill laughed a little and asked, "What, are you his secretary or something now?"

The only thing he heard was a bit of static. He thought maybe she had thrown the radio. Right away, Terry picked up on his radio. "Terry here. What's up?"

Watching Danny while he spoke, Bill told him, "I need you to get in here. Bring your kit with you. There is an injured person in here. You must be unarmed. Come through the front door and move to the back of the building and come about halfway down the wall and wait by the door there. I will tell you what to do next."

Terry responded with, "Yes, Sir, be right in there."

Bill looked at Danny, who nodded her approval of the conversation.

While they waited, Danny asked, "Why did he call you, Sir like that?"

Bill lowered his head as he replied, "Because I was an officer in the Army, but I recently retired. Being in the military, as some of my group was, they have taken to calling me like that."

She seemed to accept the explanation and appeared to relax a little, but kept the rifle pointed in his direction.

It didn't take Terry long before he got there. They could hear him as he came through the door and made his way back along the wall. Suddenly, it was all quiet. After a brief wait, Terry yelled out, "Okay, I'm here. What now?"

Bill held up the radio, and Danny nodded. Keying it up, he told Terry, "Slowly come through the door. When you get inside, set your kit down and lay on the floor, with your face down, and don't move. They will give you instructions after that."

He set the radio down when he remembered. "Move slowly all the time. They will have you covered."

Terry came in and went through the same drill Bill had. When they were both sitting side by side against the wall, Terry asked, "Who is the one that is injured?"

Bill pointed to Danny and said, "She is. The kids have wrapped her leg, but they think she broke it."

Terry turned to Danny and, pointing to her foot, and he asked, "May I look at it?"

Again, Danny jerked the rifle up, and this time, Terry froze. Speaking slowly, Terry explained, "I can't do anything with it all wrapped up that way. If you broke it, I'm going to need to touch you to see how bad it might be." However, before she could answer, he added, "And I don't work very well with guns pointed at me."

It was now a standoff. Danny would have to trust Terry enough to let him check her leg, or she would have to let the kids continue to treat her. Her son leaned forward and whispered in her ear.

Danny thought before turning answering Terry to say, "Alright, you can check it out." She handed the rifle to her son. The boy took the gun that was much too big for him to handle correctly.

Bill tried to say something, but the boy swung the rifle in his direction. Putting his hands up again, Bill said to his mother, "I will not put my man in danger. If he touches you and you jump, your son might jump and shoot him. I can't let that happen. Either you trust us or let us go."

After thinking a moment, Danny motioned for her son to put the rifle down and sit on the other bed.

Terry slowly moved forward and lifted Danny's leg. He took a pair of scissors out and cut her pant leg up to the knee. Slowly, he unwrapped the leg. As he got down to the ankle, they both could see the color of her skin change. When the wrap was entirely off, Terry leaned over with a flashlight and examined her carefully. He felt up the leg, and there was no reaction from Danny. As he touched around the ankle, she jumped and let out a hiss. Stopping there, Terry finished by checking her foot.

Sitting back, Terry announced, "Well, I don't believe your leg is broken."

The little girl jumped up and came over to hug her mother.

Terry added, "That was the good news. The bad news is, I think your ankle might be broken. We don't have an x-ray machine, and it is too tender for me to touch, but from the looks of everything, it is my judgment that you broke it."

Bill asked, "What can we do about it?"

Thinking, Terry said, "There should be an x-ray in the local hospital, but that doesn't help without power. We need to go to the hospital and get some stuff to make a cast. I can also get Novocain and give her a shot while trying to set and cast it."

Danny asked, "Just how do you think you're going to get me to a hospital? I can't walk."

Bill laughed, saying, "That won't be a problem. We are at a fire station. They are bound to have a way to move you. If not, we'll simply put you on a cot. There are enough of us to get you there."

"Why don't you drive me there in the ambulance or another car?" She asked.

It hit Bill. She still doesn't know what is happening. He sat down on the bunk next to her and told her the situation. "You don't realize what is happening yet." He started with. Tuning to Terry, he said, "Terry, will you take the kids out and see if you can find something that we can use to transport Danny to the hospital? Take your time and introduce them to the rest of the group."

Terry nodded and appeared to understand that Bill wanted time to explain. Talking to the kids, he asked, "Do you guys know where they might have a cart or stretcher? We need to put your mom on it?"

The boy stood up and said, "I think so. Come on. I'll show you."

As they were leaving the room, Bill heard Terry ask what their names were. He heard the boy say his name was Sam. The door closed before he could hear the girl's answer, so he looked at Danny and showed he didn't hear it.

She said, "Her name is Susan."

"Sam and Susan." Bill echoed back. "Nice names. They seem like great kids."

"They are. They've been asking where their father is, but I don't know what to tell them. I keep saying he went for help."

Bill stared at the floor when she started talking about their father. She must have seen something was wrong. She leaned forward and asked, "What's the matter? What aren't you telling me?"

He explained, as he watched her face. "I'm afraid it is probably not good news. It started about two weeks ago."

Bill went through the entire story about his group and what they had seen and what they have figured out so far.

She didn't say a word until he finished. Bill thought she might be in shock from all this strange news. She sat there, staring at the floor and shaking her head.

Finally, she asked the obvious question, "How can you be sure?"

Bill responded with a simple, "Because we have seen the alien creatures."

Again, she sat shaking her head and said, "That's not possible."

Bill nodded, saying, "I'm afraid it is possible, and the results are, we may be the only ones left. We have been monitoring short wave radio and so far, have we've not heard from anyone else."

There was a long silence before the children came back with Terry. The kids were excited to announce they found a stretcher for their mom. The excitement quickly went away when they saw their mother. Sam came up to her and asked, "What the matter, mom?"

She stared at her son and her daughter. Before she could answer, a tear formed in her eyes. "Sit down. I need to talk to both of you."

Bill turned to leave, but Danny grabbed his hand and asked, "Please stay. I may need your help to get through this."

Bill gave her his best comforting look and sat back down, this time on the other bunk. He wanted to give her kids enough room to be with their mom.

Danny went through the complete story again with the kids. Sometimes she glanced at Bill, and he filled in the details. It was terrible when they discussed what might have happened to their father.

Susan asked Bill, "Do you think it hurt my father when they killed him?"

Bill tried to comfort her with a smile and told her, "No, from what I saw, I don't think it hurt anyone. It was over very quickly."

Susan buried her head in her mom's lap and cried for a while.

After a while, Bill asked Danny, "I think we had better get moving. It is not advisable to travel at night. The hospital is very close to where we have made a community. I would like to suggest that after we get you patched up, we take you to our place and give you time to heal and decide what to do next."

Both of her kids appeared to like the idea. Bill thought they might need a lot more of a social connection than they were getting here.

Danny said, with the first smile he had seen on her face, "I think we would like that."

Bill told the kids, "Go grab your stuff. Only bring what you absolutely need. It is going to be a long walk to my place, and you're going to have to carry whatever you bring."

Sam got right to it and started shoving stuff into a backpack. Susan was a little slower to respond and needed a little guidance from mom, but she packed quickly.

The rest of the team came in, and Danny was a little worried until Casey came in. She saw the State Trooper on the back of her jacket and relaxed a little. They got Danny on the stretcher and gathered as many of the supplies as each of them could carry. They slowly made their way to the hospital.

At the hospital, Casey took her team back to the cave while Bill stayed with Danny and her kids. He and Ahmed kept the kids busy while Terry took care of their mother. He took the kids to search the hospital for things like crutches and wheelchairs. They also searched for other supplies and food. By the time they gathered stuff and stashed it near the front doors to come back for later, Terry had finished with their mother. This time they loaded her in a wheelchair but also brought crutches for her.

On the way back to the cave, they saw a distant speck in the sky but didn't take any chances. They quickly got Danny on the ground and covered, while the kids also took cover with extra thermal blankets. The alien craft soon disappeared, and they continued to make their way to the cave with no further trouble.

Casey had told everyone what they found. When Bill got back with Danny and the kids, everyone had gathered near the stairs to welcome them. BJ and Nancy were at the front of the crowd and ran up to Danny's kids right away. It was a friendship right away, especially with Nancy and Susan, when the puppy came into play.

They slowly went back into the main chamber, where the ladies set up a special meal. Somebody had already set up a place with a tent for the newcomers, and soon everyone gathered to eat.

Bill thought that the question about adding people to the group was now answered, at least for now.

As time went by, the group continued gathering supplies and searching the area for others. First, they found a young woman by herself and accepted her into the group. There was another man they saw, but the group responsible for finding him watched for several hours. By the way, he was armed and acted made them nervous. He appeared to be more interested in weapons and riches than anything else. They decided not to contact him, and he eventually went on his way north.

Early in the morning, one day, when Bill woke up, he made his daily rounds in the cave to check on things before anyone else was up. When he checked in with the watch at the cave opening, he found Casey on duty. She was further out into the opening than typical and was keeping an eye to the west. Bill grabbed a blanket they kept by the entrance and went out to join her.

As he approached, Casey acknowledged him. Bill sat next to her and stared out in the direction she had been watching. Without looking at her, he asked, "What's going on?"

Casey pointed to an area toward Walmart and explained, "About two hours ago, I spotted one of their craft slowly coming this way from the south. As it went by, I came out to watch it. It appears to have landed out past the Walmart, near that airport or golf course."

She let Bill think a bit, but added, "I think it is still there. I've been watching and didn't see it take off again."

Bill sat back for a moment but kept scanning in that direction. Finally, after a while, he asked her, "What do you make of it?"

Casey didn't reply right away and took her time to think about her answer. Finally, she said, "I don't know what's going on. Watching this craft, I thought it was the first time I can recall, after the beginning, that they have come around this way and showed any interest in anything."

After a moment, she added, "I'm just curious about what it is doing over there."

Bill was in full agreement and replied, "Me too. I'm going to get Tom and maybe someone else, and we'll head over there and check around." He asked, "Are you too tired, or are you interested in coming along?"

Casey swung around to him to show a big smile. "Oh, you can bet I'm in. I wouldn't miss this for the world."

As he got up to leave, he said, "Keep watching it, and I'll be right back with the others."

Casey quickly gave him a thumbs up and went back to her watch.

Bill went back to the main area and found Tom and Ahmed. They were finishing breakfast when he saw them. Calling them together, he asked, "Do you two feel up to a patrol? Something interesting happened this morning, and I feel we need to go check it out."

Tom spoke up right away. "You bet."

Ahmed pointed to his wife, who was still sitting where they were eating breakfast. Back to Bill, he asked, "Do I have time to speak to my wife?"

Bill smiled when he answered, "Certainly, in fact, I need to check in with my wife." However, before the other two could leave, he added, "Make sure you're armed. Preferably with automatic weapons."

This last statement got a serious look from the two men, but they simply nodded as they slowly left. Bill could see that the last part had them thinking.

Bill went to his family area and woke his wife to explain what was happening. When he finished, Judy had a stern expression on her face and told him, "I don't like the sound of this. We don't know what these things are capable of or what they will do."

This time Bill kept a serious look about him as he responded to her worry, "Yes, I agree, but this is the first time we might be able to get a good idea of what they are up to. We really need to do this. I plan to stay far away and watch them."

Judy had that look that says, I know that is your plan, but not what you will do.

This time, Bill took her by the shoulders and smiled. "It will be alright. We won't do anything stupid."

Judy smiled back. However, the expression that was still there said she didn't believe him.

Bill got up to leave when he heard BJ's soft voice say, "Be careful, Dad."

"Don't worry, I will," Bill said as he smiled at his son. Nancy was still sleeping, but he smiled at her, anyway.

As he left his family, Bill went over to their weapons area, picked up one of the fully automatic M-16's they got from the police station, and headed out to meet up with the others.

When he got to the opening, he found Tom had another of the M-16's, and Ahmed was following him with a semi-AK they found in an empty home.

Shortly, Casey's relief showed up. After a quick check for ammo, water, and food, they started making their way in the direction Casey had been watching. Because she saw where the craft went down, Bill had her take point to lead the way.

There were no incidents on the way. They made good time getting to Walmart. From there, they were a lot more careful. There was a trail behind the store that led to a small group of houses next to the airport. When they got to the edge of the woods and could see the airport, and backtracked to come up between the houses. That was going to get them the closest so they could see.

Since this all began, they all had been on many patrols together. Now they were acting like a well-trained military unit. They slowly closed in on the airport. Once they were behind the last houses, Bill took out his binoculars and scanned the area. From this position, he saw nothing unusual. He also checked the golf course, or as much of it as he could see, which wasn't much. There was nothing.

Getting back out of sight, he called Casey on the radio to ask, "Are you sure this is the area you saw the craft in?"

Confidently, she answered, "Yes, in this area, but I can't say the exact site. It could also have hovered above the ground as it moved. I wouldn't have been able to see that."

Bill thought for a moment and took another quick check. Finally, he radioed, "Alright, we're going to have to move to get a better look. If we move south to the bend in the road, it should give us a better view down the field."

He heard, "Copy." Replies three times. He led the way back to the cover of the houses and moved south. When he found a spot with trees and bushes that were close to the road, he again signaled to stop and take cover.

This spot offered little better view, but it allowed him to find a ditch they could use to get to the fence, unseen, and cut their way through. He called on the radio, "Who has the wire cutters?"

Tom replied, "I've got them."

Bill instructed Tom. "You see that ditch, right across from me?" He didn't wait for a response but continued. "I want you to make your way across the road and up to the fence. Cut a low crawl through for us and wait on the other side, out of sight."

Tom responded with a simple, "Copy."

Bill watched as Tom made his way to complete the assignment. It was an agonizingly slow process, but he made it. After he was through, Tom waved back to Bill that he was ready. Bill keyed up his radio and called "Casey."

She did not respond, but Bill could see her move. Her low crawl across the road was not too good, and as he watched, Bill made a mental note to work on that with her.

Before he could call Ahmed, Bill saw he was on the move. Bill could see the practiced movements he had gained from a lifetime of living in dangerous areas. He completed his move to the site. As they all got through the fence, Tom assigned a direction for each of them to watch.

Bill now checked the skies before he moved. Seeing everything was clear, he made his way to join the group. As he emerged from under the fence, Tom signaled his attention and gave the sign that he saw something and pointed to the hangar area.

Bill continued his low crawl to where Tom was and pulled out the binoculars. He found he didn't need them because he could see what might be the top of an alien craft parked between the two buildings. It didn't appear to be moving. Judging by the height of the hangers, it must be sitting on the ground.

Bill studied the layout for a moment. He saw a slope, and the hill peaked very close to the hangar buildings. So, he began thinking that if they could get close to the peak, they would get a good look at that thing.

Bill slid back down into the ditch. As Tom came down beside him, Bill asked, "Did you see it?"

There was a round of agreements from everyone.

Bill sat there a while and motioned for Tom to continue to watch. He was content to watch and see what happened, but an idea came into his thoughts about trying to catch this thing. If they could learn to communicate, they might find out what is happening.

Bill studied the group and motioned them to gather close. When they were all together, he whispered this idea. "What do you think about trying to catch this thing? We could learn a lot if we can communicate with it."

Tom said nothing, but Bill could see he was thinking very hard about the idea.

Casey whispered back, "I don't know if that's such a good idea. We know nothing about what they are capable of doing." After a second thought, she quickly added, "With or without weapons."

Bill glanced at Ahmed, but he continued watching the building where the alien was. Bill finally called his name, and that brought him back to the conversation. He slowly started talking. "Casey is correct. We know nothing about them."

Casey smiled at Bill.

However, Ahmed continued, "And if we don't get in contact with them, we never will."

Bill stared at Casey. She gave him the very slightest of a nod. However, it was clear she was not happy with the idea.

This time, he didn't smile at her. Instead, he wanted to show how serious he was when he answered her, "You and Ahmad are both right. We know nothing about them. All of us can't live the rest of our lives in a cave. If there's any chance for our survival, we need to get one of those things and learn to communicate with it."

She shot right back at him. "What if he has a ray gun or something? How are you going to deal with something like that? Remember those people who simply disappeared?"

"Yes, I fully remember. However, this is the first time we have seen one get out and look around or do anything since that first sighing. I'm saying if we want the human race to continue, we are going to have to take this opportunity to do something."

Everyone was quiet for a long while. Bill was thinking he had lost this fight over what to do. He didn't want to push them to make up their minds, but they were running out of time. They had to act now.

Checking with Tom, he asked, "What do you say?"

Tom didn't look at him right away but continued to watch toward the hangers. Finally, he turned his head back to say, "The way you put it, I can see this is something we must do. I don't like it, though."

Bill scanned the ground before he responded, and with a smile, he replied, "I'm not crazy about the idea of disappearing, either. I don't have a death wish. That is why we must do it to ensure we can all live on."

Next, Bill glanced at Ahmed. Without a word, he responded with a thumbs up.

Last, Bill waited on Casey. She was shaking her head, and Bill thought he would lose her because of this issue. After a long moment, Casey also nodded her agreement with this plan.

Bill now laid out his plan, starting with Tom. "I want you to make your way around what, I think is, a fueling station and the temporary hanger. You should be able to make your way up to the first hangar."

Tom scanned the route he was to take and replied, "That's going to leave me out in the open if anything breaks."

"That's why Ahmed is going to follow you and stay low. He should be able to monitor you while staying out of sight from the other hangar."

Before everyone moved out, he added, "Keep off the radios as much as possible. Move to your positions. I'll finish the plan and radio it when Casey and I get to the top and get an eye on things. Do not respond and keep the volume low." He moved but quickly added, "Remember, we want this thing alive and preferably unharmed. However, your safety comes first. Kill if you must, and we'll all get the hell out of here, fast."

Nobody responded as they all started crawling on their bellies as low as they could get. Tom went off to the left, and shortly Ahmed followed him. Bill and Casey kept a distance between them and painstakingly made their way up the slight incline that was the hill. Even though this was barely a hill, Bill couldn't remember a more challenging climb in all his army career.

When Bill and Casey got high enough to see the area. He could now see the entire alien craft sitting on the ground between the two rows of hangers. It was the same as the one they saw on the first day. However, this one still had the door ramp open. Bill thought about the excellent opportunity to peek inside to gather some information, but decided this was not the time for that. Their best source of information is the creature driving that thing. Again, checking the buildings, Bill saw a couple of old semi-trailers parked at this end. He motioned for Casey to make her way to the trailers and take up a position there.

Casey simply nodded and started crawling along the ridge to get closer.

While she was on the move, Bill tried to check out the status of the others. Tom was at the fulling station, but Ahmed was out of sight. So, Bill guessed he was right behind Tom on the other side of the building.

Bill used hand signals to tell Tom to move of the building on the left and take up a position there. With Casey and Tom in those positions, it would give them a very good crossfire on whatever that thing was.

Bill moved down the hill when everyone was in place, taking cover behind the other semi-trailer to wait. But no sooner than Bill got into position, he heard the door from the second hangar down open. He saw one of the alien creatures come out of a hangar. It went across to the other building, and after playing with the door a moment, it went in. He quickly got on the ground and slid under the trailer to take up a position behind the tires, where he had a splendid view to cover the area. From here, he could still see the craft sitting there with the door ramp still down on the ground. Bill continued to watch, and after a while, he got on the radio and whispered, "We'll take him when he comes out and gets halfway across."

There was no response, and he didn't expect one. So, they all sat there and waited. Finally, after about fifteen minutes, the creature came out and glanced around. It headed back to the spaceship.

Before the creature could get more than a few steps, Bill moved out from behind the trailer. The creature continued to walk, so Bill yelled, "Hey you!"

Now the creature stopped and turned. Bill could see what he thought was fear in the alien creature. As Bill moved towards the thing, he motioned for it to raise its hands. It was apparent that it did not understand. Bill shifted the rifle to the one hand and used more direct indicators. This time, the creature understood and raised its pencil-thin arms above its head.

Bill was now close enough to get a good view of this thing. It didn't appear to be wearing any clothes. Even so, Bill could not see any distinguishing body features. There were gigantic eyes and a small slit, he thought, might be a mouth. But no discernable nose or ears. Also, there was no navel or no genitals visible.

Bill walked toward the creature, with his rifle still at the ready. The creature didn't move and only continued to stare at him with those big eyes. Finally, when he was a few feet away from it, Bill stopped. They both stood there, staring at each other for a little while. Bill spoke, "Do you understand our language?"

The creature didn't respond. It didn't move, and there was no change in the expressionless face.

Again, they stared at each other after a little Bill called the rest of his team in. As Casey came into view, the creature's eyes moved to glance at her, but right back to Bill. When Tom and Ahmed came around the building, the creature turned its whole body slightly to see them. Bill realized this thing had limited head movement and needed to turn its body to see them.

As the last two joined the group in a circle around the alien, it again faced Bill. It was as if this creature knew he was in charge of the group. They needed to get out of the area quickly and back to their cave. Bill motioned for the creature to move. When it didn't, Tom got behind it and gave it a push with the muzzle of his rifle. It turned around and appeared to sneer at Tom, but Tom did nothing more. As the creature turned back to Bill, it stopped while looking in the craft's direction. Suddenly, the door ramp retracted, and the ship shot straight up into the sky and was out of sight in seconds. The creature completed its turn and started walking in the direction that Bill had initially shown.

For a second, the group stood there, shot glances around at each other, and followed the creature. Tom took the lead. At the fence, he cut a big enough hole for the alien to get through. They continued back to the cave without a single incident.

Bill stopped the group near the top of the stairs. He had the alien sit down. That was a little difficult to get across to it, but once it understood what Bill wanted, it kind of folded its legs up under it as it went down. It reminded Bill of an enormous bowling pin when it sat there. To the group, he said, "Tom, I want you and Casey to head back in and join the group. Have them all gather at the talking stage. Don't tell them anything about our guest. I want to see the reaction of each of them when it walks into the room. This will tell us who we might have trouble with later. Ahmed and I will follow in about ten minutes."

Both Tom and Casey smiled as they turned to leave. They knew the surprise that was going is coming. When they were out of sight, Bill went back up a couple of steps and sat down on the opposite side of the creature. Again, they sat there silently, staring at each other.

Ahmed had been sitting a little lower down the stairs, watching. Finally, after about ten minutes, he made a slight cough and called Bill. He had to call him two times before he responded. Ahmed showed his watch and motioned down the hall to the main area.

Bill motioned with his rifle for the alien to get up, and it slowly and effortlessly regained a standing position. Bill didn't think the thing could move like that, given the size of the body to the limbs. However, he quickly shook that off and motioned for the creature to move down the Before they got to the main chamber, Bill said, "Stop." When everyone stopped, he kept his eyes on the creature as he moved around to whisper to Ahmed, "We need to protect this thing from the others. Some may be angry, but we don't want to kill or hurt any of our people. Clear."

Ahmed added, "That may not be very easy to do."

Bill glanced back at him and nodded an agreement. He went back behind the alien and nudged it with his rifle. They moved again. It was only a few seconds before they entered the main chamber. Bill could see Tom and Casey on the stage, and all the people gathered around. There was talk among the people, but when Tom looked up as Bill came in, immediately, all talking stopped. There were a few gasps of disbelief, but no one move toward the alien. Bill cautiously moved the creature toward the people, but stopped a few yards away. He came around to the front and motioned for Ahmed to go behind it.

Everyone stood there for a moment. Bill waved for Tom and Casey to come back down with him. Once there, Bill walked up and took his place on the stage. A few people turned towards him, but most continued to stare at the creature. Bill waited a moment before speaking, "Ladies and Gentlemen, may I have your attention, please." The rest of the people slowly focused on him. When he saw all the eyes were on him, he continued, "As you can see, we have captured one of the alien creatures that invaded our world." His words got a round of nodes and comments of agreement. "I plan to learn how to communicate with it and find out as much information as I can."

Bill was not ready for the response he got from many in the group. Finally, someone shouted, "Information, Hell. Kill the damn thing as they did to our families."

Another person called out, "This may be our only chance to seek some revenge. Kill it now."

Bill could not tell who was saying what. All the people were talking at the same time. He held up his hands to get their attention, but only a few responded. Finally, he had to shout, but it wasn't until Casey fired a round into a wall that everyone stopped. Bill quickly retook control of the talk. "People, we can't just kill this thing. We must find out what is going on. This group cannot move ahead with our lives if we don't have information. We need a dialog with them. If we cannot communicate with them, we have no chance of surviving for very long."

His people had now calmed down. There were still murmurings going on, but nobody appeared to be upset right now. Bill let this go on a little while before he tried again to talk. "I intend to communicate with this thing and see what information we can get from it." As he watched, Bill saw a couple of men he didn't know leaving the group and heading towards the armory. Tom took up a position between them and the arsenal, with his rifle held at the ready. As the men closed in, Casey moved around to the group's rear and took up a position there. Ahmed was now standing in front of the alien to protect it. There was a standoff for a minute, but the men retreated to the sleeping area. Bill was sure this would not be the end.

Bill's attention was now back on the group in front of him. A woman's voice, he recognized the voice to be Danny, shouted out, "I want you to find out what happened to my husband."

All he could do was nod an agreement. He held up his hands to say, "I will find out what happened to all the people and why the attack. But don't expect quick results. The first thing we need to do is to teach it our language. To teach it enough to get any meaningful information will take time,"

Nobody said anything more, and the group slowly broke up. As the crowd thinned, Bill saw the one thing he had been dreading since he walked back into the room. Judy was standing there with her arms crossed. She didn't move as the people left, but only stood there and stared at him. Bill knew what was coming. He slowly moved down off the talking platform and went to her. He had his head down like a dog that knows it did something wrong and was waiting for the punishment.

Before saying anything, she shifted her weight from one foot to the other and put her hands on her hips. Sarcastically, she said, "Not going to do something stupid, you said."

He recognized the tone in her voice. Bill replied, "I don't think it was really that stupid. It was more of a necessary thing we had to do."

"Stupid." That was the only thing she said back to him.

Before she could say more, Bill added, "The others agreed with the idea."

Judy threw up her hands and made a sound he was all too familiar with when she knew she had lost the fight. She quickly stormed off to the ladies' room. All Bill could do was watch until she was out of sight.

After he recovered from the encounter with his wife, Bill's attention was back to the alien. His team had moved back to guard it and was standing there. Bill wasn't sure if they heard the encounter with his wife, so he didn't know what to say, going back to join them.

As he walked up, Bill started the conversation so they couldn't say anything about what happened. "We need a safe place to keep this thing while we try to communicate. I want a guard on it at all times." He paused a moment as he thought, but added, "I think we also need a guard on the armory."

Tom stepped forward to say, "That's an awful lot of guarding for just the four of us."

"Yes, but if we keep it near the armory, one person can guard both, plus I don't expect we will need to do this for very long."

Tom agreed, but the others didn't show whether or not they agreed. Bill didn't wait for any more talk. Instead, he motioned for them to follow as he headed towards the armory area.

Near the armory, there was a small alcove. Bill stepped inside to check around. It was big enough to hold the alien and very close to the armory. He stated to the others, "This will be perfect."

Ahmed nudged the creature in the back and motioned for it to go inside.

Once inside, the alien made a complete turn and went to the far side and did its sitting down routine. Now it sat there, staring at the group, but still appeared to be focused mostly on Bill.

Bill said, "One of you stays to guard it. I don't care who. Draw straws or something. Swap out during the night, and we'll start seeing what we can do with it in the morning. But first, I need to go smooth things out with the Boss."

As he started to leave, Casey spoke up. "You can start by telling her the truth. Not all of us agreed that this was a smart thing to do!"

Bill didn't really respond to what she said and stood there. Quickly, Casey realized he knew she was right and smiled at him and walked away.

When Bill returned to his family's sleeping area, he found Nancy and BJ were already asleep. He checked inside the little tent that he a Judy shared, and she also appeared to be sleeping. Not wanting to wake her up to start a conversation he didn't want; Bill found a quiet spot to sit and think. It wasn't long before he, also, was sleeping.

CHAPTER

7

Bill was still half asleep when he heard someone telling him, *"Wake up, Major Jenson."*

As he rolled over, he opened his eyes. Suddenly, he became very disoriented. Nothing was right. There were no soldiers around, and he was not in uniform. Quickly, he came out of it and looked around. He was still in the cave, and everything was quiet. Thinking to himself that it must have been a dream, he laid back down and closed his eyes.

No sooner than his eyes closed, he heard the voice again saying, *"Wake up!"*

Bill now jumped up to his feet and glanced around. There was no one there. It sounded like the voice was right near his head, but there was nobody around. Checking the kids, he found they were still sleeping and crawling over to peer into the tent. He found Judy was still asleep.

Now he was up and wide awake. Something was not right, but he couldn't put a finger on it right now. He figured if he was up, he might as well relieve himself. After going to the men's room, he went back to his bed to get some more sleep. He nearly jumped five feet when he heard the voice again, right behind him, *"Come see me."* Bill quickly swung around in a circle, and there was no one there.

For some reason he couldn't understand, he went over the see if the alien was alright. As he walked to the alcove, he kept turning around to make sure nobody was near or following him. Once he got there, he found Ahmed sitting up against the wall, sleeping.

Stopping, he shook his head and went to wake him up to scold him about sleeping on duty. As Bill was reaching down to grab Ahmed's shoulder, he heard the voice again. *"Let him sleep."*

Bill swung around with his back to the wall so hard he hit his head on a rock. He felt the spot, but there was no blood, but it hurt. Carefully checking all around, he found no one around. After a moment, he peeked into the alcove, and the alien was still sitting where he had left him hours ago. Like before, it was staring at Bill again. And again, there was the voice, *"Yes, it is me who is calling to you."*

Bill ducked back around the corner with his back to the wall to think for a minute. However, this time, he was careful not to hit his head. Slowly, he peered around the edge to see the alien. It was still sitting there, staring at him. Bill slowly walked into the room. When he was halfway to the alien, he heard the voice say, *"Please sit down. We have much to talk about."*

He moved to an opposite wall, and as he sat down, a million questions were running through his head. He didn't know where to start.

The voice was gentle and polite. It spoke softly and clearly, *"Yes, I can talk directly to your mind. I can also understand what you are thinking. My people have developed this form of communication and have learned to control it. It makes communicating with less developed species like you possible."*

"How is this possible?" It was Bill's first thought, but he quickly thought how ridiculous this question was and asked, "What is it you want from us?"

The simple reply that came into his head was, *"Nothing."*

The answer shocked Bill. He couldn't understand. Speaking out loud, he asked, "Then why have you killed almost all the people?"

The alien replied, *"No one has died since we came to your world."*

Again, Bill was more confused now. He thought about the first time he saw one of the alien crafts and how it disintegrated all those people. However, before he could ask about it, the alien spoke into his mind again, *"Those people were not killed. We have simply taken them. They are sleeping aboard our ships."*

Before Bill could speak his next question, the alien was again in his head with the answer, *"I can hear your question as it is formulated in your mind. So, before you can speak, I have already sent the answer directly into your brain."*

Bill sat there, thinking for a moment. Everything was all happening too fast. Softly, the voice continued, *"Give it time. You will quickly learn how much better this form of communication is. You cannot control it as we do. It took us many generations to get to this level."*

Bill sat there, stunned. He didn't know what to ask or even say. Again, the creature spoke to his mind, *"I was sent here to teach you and prepare you for your new future. Soon, I will send you and the others short bursts of information. It will be impossible for you to understand everything at once. These little bursts will give your primitive minds time to understand and organize in your mind and not overload you."*

Bill thought for a moment and nodded to the creature. The creature added, *"You may call me by the name John. It will make it easier for you."*

Bill smiled as he thought it was much better than calling him, It or Creature.

The voice replied, *"Yes, I agree."*

Bill's head suddenly cleared. He glanced around as if he had come out of a dream. John, was still staring at him.

Slowly, Ahmed started waking up. He stirred a little and jumped up when he realized he had been sleeping. Seeing Bill sitting there, he asked, "When did you come here?"

Bill didn't answer him right away. His mind was still going through everything John had told him. He glanced over at John, who sat there staring at him. Suddenly, Bill stood and walked out when he remembered Ahmed. Stopping, he looked at him and calmly said, "Stay awake on duty."

Before Ahmed could say anything, Bill left. Heading back out to the main chamber, he first went over to the food area and grabbed coffee and checked on his family. Since they were still sleeping, he went deeper into the cave to find a place to think. Finding a somewhat comfortable rock, he sat down and sipped at his coffee. He smiled as he remembered the first time he tried this coffee. It had gotten much better now they were using bottled water to make it.

Bill started going through all the things that happened this morning. First, he wanted to test to see how far the alien, John's power to read minds, went. Before he could even form the question in his mind, the answer came back as clear as if John was sitting right next to him, *"Yes, I can still hear you."*

Bill spoke out loud. "You need to stop peeking into my private thoughts. We would consider this to be rude."

The voice came back, *"As you wish, but once I break the link, you cannot talk to me again unless I call you or you come to see me."*

"That would be fine, for now. I need time to think," Bill said and quickly added, "In private."

The instant he said it, something was missing from his head. His mind felt as if something had let go. He had no actual way to test if John was still listening or not. He had to go by his feeling that John had left his head.

Bill sat and drank his coffee as he tried to organize his thinking into a reasonable plan to explain to his people. He was deep in his thoughts when he heard noises coming from the community area. Grabbing his cup, he ran back to the main room. He found a small group of, primarily men, armed with sticks and anything else they could grab. It appeared they were trying to get at John. Ahmed, Tom, and Casey were all lined up against the group. Bill couldn't see Terry, and that was a little troublesome. He needed to know if all his team was with him.

Bill walked up behind the group of men and shouted, "What's going on here?"

Some men jumped. He noted those. They were the nervous ones and not sure this is what they should be doing. The rest, however, turned to him and started shouting. One man walked up to the front to face Bill. Bill remembered him as the man who left the group in a rage yesterday. He had an iron crowbar in his hands.

While remaining calm, Bill asked, "What's going on? Do you plan on killing our only hope of survival?"

"You tell him, Will." Came the shouts from other men who were standing right behind him.

Will stood up straighter and, with a self-righteous tone, shouted, "You're damn right. We plan to get a little retribution for our family that it killed."

Bill could smell the alcohol on Will's breath. Most of these men must have been up all night, drinking themselves into this mob. Still, Bill remained calm as he responded, "Is that right. What if I told you that your families are not dead? And then you kill it. That might put an end to your families, and you would be the only one to hold the blame."

This idea took Will back a step. After a moment, he took another step forward to ask, "How do you know these things?"

Bill smugly replied, "Because I took the time to learn to talk to him."

Now, the men who had been following Will seemed less determined. They dropped their arms, and their weapons now hung by their sides. A couple of those who had initially jumped when Bill spoke, took a few steps back. Still, none of them said anything. It was Will that spoke up. Still angry, he shouted, "Is that what that thing in there said to you?"

In Bill's head, he heard John again, *"Yes."*

It startled Bill, but the rest of those men began looking at each other and around behind them. They were doing the same thing Bill had done when he first heard that voice. Except now, he couldn't help but smile."

Will stared at Bill. Letting him think about it a moment, Bill finally said, "Yes, that was the alien. He is talking directly into your brain, or whatever you call that pile of shit growing inside your head."

Will said nothing. He continued to stand there. Again, Bill heard John, <u>"Tell them to go back to your talking area, and I will come out and talk to all of them shortly."</u>

None of the men moved this time, so Bill guessed John was only talking to him this time. With Will standing there, Bill walked past him and stood with his team. When everyone was watching him, he said, "I want all of you to return to your area. Shortly, I will bring the alien out. He will address all of you, at that time."

The men looked back and forth at each other and slowly dispersed. Will was the last to go, and as he left, he kept checking back over his shoulder at Bill.

When all the men had gone out of sight, Bill focused on his team. Tom spoke up, "That was really the alien? It sounded like he was talking right into my ear."

Before Bill could answer, Ahmed said, "He was speaking in my native language. It was so clear."

Bill smiled and said, "Follow me."

When he walked into the area where they kept the alien, Bill finally saw Terry. He had his little medical kit out and was next to John. Quickly he asked, "Terry, is he alright? What's wrong?"

"Nothing is wrong." Terry responded, "When the men came, I ran in here to see what I could find out about John, so if he got hurt, I might help him. It's amazing. In a couple of seconds, I knew all I needed to know to take care of him."

Terry had a huge smile on his face, like a little kid coming home from his first day of school. Bill smiled as he told him, "Good man. I only hope you never have to use any of that knowledge John gave you."

Casey now jumped in. "You named that thing John?"

Before Bill could say anything, Terry jumped in. "No, this is the name that he would like us to call him. It is much better if we have a name for him instead of what we've been calling him."

Casey shook her head and stepped back.

Bill shifted attention back to John and, without speaking, asked, *"What do you want to do now?"*

This time John's eyes shifted back to Bill, and he heard, *"That is excellent, Major. You have already picked up that you do not need to speak your words to me. It usually takes others longer to get the idea of this type of communication."*

Before Bill could voice his objection to John about using his former rank. John said, *"I use this title to let you know you are the leader of this group and will continue to lead them from now on. I will start calling you William from now on."*

Bill couldn't think of anything to say about what John had told him. It was too much to handle in such a short and chaotic time. Also, he didn't have time to respond. John spoke again, and seeing Tom and Casey jump, Bill knew he was talking to all of them. *"I would like to go out, and I will speak to the entire group and explain what we are doing here and what is going to happen."*

Before any of them could move, John added, *"I do not want to provoke anyone, so you will not need your weapons. I can defend myself."*

Bill first stared at John for a moment. To his team he said, "You heard him. Stow the weapon and we will form up and head out."

Before Casey could object, John added, *"Yes, Trooper Williams, you may keep your sidearm as you always do."*

As they left, Casey said to Bill, "But I didn't say anything."

Bill told her, "You don't need to say anything. He knows what you are going to say before you say it and sends the answer directly into your brain before you can even talk."

Casey stared down and mumbled, "I don't know that I like him in my head like that."

Bill laughed a little and told her, "Yea, I know what you're saying. Unnerving, isn't it?"

Once everyone was ready. The entire group moved to the main chamber. Bill was in the lead, followed by John. The rest of the team took position surrounding John. As they came into the main room, all the talking stopped. Bill continued to lead the group to the speaking platform.

Before he could get to the top of the short platform, people began to gather. It didn't take long for all the people to form a circle in front of John. Bill waited a long time before he said anything. He wanted to be sure everyone was there. Bill thought to John and asked, in his mind, *"What now?"*

John took up his usual setting position and watched the crowd that had gathered. Bill heard in his head, *"We need to wait a little longer. There are two females in the other room to relieve themselves."*

Bill smiled, but turned back to the group. While they waited, he scanned the group. Finding most of the men they had encountered last night standing off to the side near the ramp leading up to the platform. Bill's military mind kicked in. He saw how these men had placed themselves in a position that would let them overrun the platform before anyone could react. Nodding to Tom, Bill showed the group of men. Tom moved to the top of the ramp to take up a defensive position.

In his head, Bill heard John say, *"That was a good call. Those men plan to do harm to me. However, your moving of Sargent Ballard was unnecessary. I can defend myself. When the time is right, I will show you and everyone here they cannot harm me."*

Bill only continued to watch the crowd, just as the two ladies came out of the ladies' room. They stopped when they saw everyone gathered and the alien up on the platform. Slowly, they moved to join the group and find their husbands.

To get their attention, Bill raised up his hands. Once it was quiet, he announced, "Our guest would like to talk to everyone. He can speak directly into your mind and in whatever language you are most comfortable with. To make matters simple, he would like us to refer to him as John."

Bill stepped back to leave John alone in the front. Before he could start, the group of men made their move. They hadn't even taken two steps when Bill heard John say one word, *"Pain."*

Suddenly, all the men in that group dropped to the floor. Some were down on their knees while the other went flat on the ground. All of them were holding their abdomens while moving around in pain.

After a little, John again said one word, *"Stop."*

The men stopped with moans and groans. Slowly, and with effort, they all stood. Bill could hear John speak. *"Let this be a warning. I can make it even more painful in the future if there is any attempt to harm me or anyone here with me."*

Bill watched as the men slowly broke up, and each of them appeared to head back to a loved one. Now Bill thought to John, *"Was that necessary? They might have been hurt."*

In his mind, Bill heard, *"Yes, I needed to show an example to them and all the others, a little of what we can do. It will make things go easier in the future."*

Bill couldn't argue with the logic behind the actions and returned to his position behind John.

With none of the niceties that most humans expect from a speaker, John began, *"As William said, you can refer to me as John."*

CHAPTER

8

All the people jumped and looked around for who was speaking. John waited until they settled before he continued. *"Yes, you will need time to get used to this form of communication. It will not take you long. My people come from a distant planet. We came to this planet eons ago. We gave your ancient civilizations aid and direction."*

Bill heard someone say out loud, "I knew it."

John continued. *"We started your civilized world, gave you enough intelligence and skills to build your race. We continued to aid you and give you directions until we were called home for other reasons. Your planet became lost to our world. The experiment we started has only recently resurfaced."*

John stopped with this news. The people began thinking. Bill already had questions. A few hands went up, and there was a lot of murmuring. After a while, the arms got tired, and they soon lowered them, and the talking ceased. John went on, *"Yes, George, you are right. Many of the stories you heard on your primitive communication machine, the TV, are correct. But they do not give the complete story."*

Again, John stopped. Bill thought it might be a way of not overloading everyone's mind.

Bill heard John's voice, *"Yes."*

Suddenly, out of the crowd, a man pushed his way to the front. Scowling at John. He shouted, "How the hell do you know my name?"

John glanced down at him and said to all minds, *"Because you told me in your mind."*

It took George aback, and he said nothing more. He merely stood there with his head hanging down.

John continued. *"We found promise in your race of beings. We have come back to restart the experiment and guide you into a future with us among the stars."*

Now almost everyone's hand shot up this time. Bill stepped forward, and although John could probably handle the question, not everyone had his skill at this mind talking. So, to slow things down, he took the questions one by one. First, he pointed to a lady in the front.

She asked, "You say no one has died since you got here, but some of us say they saw people disappear? Would you please explain?"

John's voice came through loud and clear. *"We needed to find out which people are fit enough to continue life with us. They will not receive the training you will get, and we will move them to do other work. We will handle those people who have developed social or mental problems differently. If their problems can not be corrected, they will need to be destroyed."*

"Destroyed?" came out of the mouths of several people.

With unflinching confidence, John answered, *"Yes, destroyed. In our society, we have learned that these types of people will lead to too much chaos. We destroyed them for the good of society."*

The lady in front asked, "How do you know if a person is good or bad?"

John replied to answer, *"It is not something we take lightly. We have specialists trained for this type of work. They can peer deep into the mind of a being and see things that even that being didn't know about themselves. Most times, we have the skill to correct these problems. Sometimes it is beyond our skill to correct. We separate these people from the others and put through a series of tests and examinations. In the end, the ones who are uncorrectable will be destroyed. This amounts to less than one percent of all the people we examine."* John ended by adding, *"You must realize this is not something against your people. All the people in our society go through the same test and examinations, with the same results."*

Having listened, the lady appeared to have her questions answered. She stepped back. Bill pointed to a man who was standing to one side. He moved a little closer to say, "you say my son is still alive. Will I ever see him again?"

When John answered, *"Yes."* The entire group released a collective breath. John continued, *"Since you captured me, I have been in contact with my people. I have all your names and information about your direct family. They are being located and immediately starting the testing."*

Someone in the back shouted out, "What about the rest of the people?"

John continued with the calm answers, *"For most of the others, life on this planet is over. We will move them. Life on this planet is going to start again."*

"What the hell does that mean?" shouted the same voice from the back.

John did not answer the question directly. Instead, he asked, *"Richard, if you are going to continue to disrupt the process here, please step to the front to be recognized."*

Slowly, a middle-aged man made his way to the front. The people parted to let him through. Once there, he didn't need to shout, but he still insisted on an answer. "Are you going to answer my question?"

"Yes, I will answer everyone's questions. Now and in the future. We will send the rest of the people we collected to other worlds. They will live out their lives and start another race of human beings that will support the greater society's needs. They, and their children, will become citizens of an unbelievably large society on thousands of worlds with unique and mixed races of people."

This explanation didn't sit right with Richard. "You mean we are to become slaves?"

Bill almost thought he heard a little emotion for John in answering this question. *"No. We do not support slavery or any other type of bondage. These people will become citizens of our society. And as they and their children grow and learn the rules and ways of this society. We have order in our society. They will also have the rights of any citizen."*

John said only to Bill, *"I think this is enough for the moment. I hear what in their minds. They are hungry and are not focusing on the issues we need to discuss."*

Bill stepped forward and raised his hands to get everyone's attention. "It is early, and most of you have not had breakfast. We are going to take a recess for a couple of hours and then meet back here again, where we will continue."

The crowd mumbled a little, but broke up. After everyone was gone, Bill and his team escorted John back to his room. After John got settled there again, Bill made his way to his family. Judy had gathered them together to get their food. Bill kissed her and lifted Nancy to hold her while he put his other arm on BJ's shoulder. Together, they went off to get food.

As they were walking, Nancy asked, "Was that really the alien that was talking in my head?"

Bill softly replied, "Yes, that was really the alien. His name is John."

"Wow." Nancy said and got a questioning scowl on her face. She asked, "How do you know if John is a boy or girl?"

Bill stopped walking. He had never directly thought about it. How do you tell? Thinking quickly to settle her mind, Bill told her, "Well, he asked us to call him John, and John is a boy's name. We just figured he was a boy."

Nancy shrugged her shoulders and said, "Oh."

Bill was relieved that it was that simple to answer her. He wasn't ready for a talk about the birds and the bees with his daughter yet. Glancing over at his wife, he found her trying to stifle a laugh. They were close enough to the food, so he put Nancy down and told the kids to get something to eat. facing Judy, he didn't even get a word out before she started laughing and said, "Quick thinking, oh fearless leader."

Bill raised his finger to scold her, but he also laughed after what she said.

After getting some food, Bill grabbed more coffee and heading over to talk to John. He found Casey on guard duty. She acknowledged his approached, but didn't say anything. Turing into the out-cove area, Bill sat on the ground across from John.

As he took a sip of his coffee, Bill heard John ask, *"Would you like me to explain the sexual aspects of my people?"*

Bill choked on his coffee, but he said, "What?" Before John could continue, Bill figured out was he was talking about. "Oh, you mean Nancy's question? No, what I told her will keep her satisfied for now."

There was no immediate reply from John. After Bill took another sip, John said, *"We will see."*

Bill didn't answer the comment. He had more important things on his mind. "How long have you known we have been hiding down here?" He asked.

With no emotion in his voice, John answered, *"Since the beginning."*

" What?" Bill said out loud. Then, back in his mind, he said, "Why did you let us go on like that?"

John told him, *"We found the qualities we were searching for in a group of people. Your people worked together to form a community, and in a brief time, you had a government running and survival plans. Yours was the first group to advance that quickly."*

Bill quickly caught something in what John said. "What do you mean in our group?"

In his normally calm voice, John replied, *"This is not the only group of people we have been watching. There are several others across your nation and many more around the world."* However, before Bill could ask more, John continued, *"We found it particularly interesting you figured out about the heat signatures. You were partly correct. Our machines use heat to detect bodies and motors running and such. However, the operators still use their normal eyes to scan the area once they arrive at the heat source."*

"Why didn't you destroy or capture us like you did the others?"

Bill's response was not what Bill expected. *"Because we are searching for a few people for special training. It needs to be a group about the size of yours. They must show superior thinking and problem-solving abilities. Above all, they must work and act as a team."*

Bill sat back for a moment and sipped at his coffee as John watched him. Suddenly, it occurred to Bill that John had not eaten or drunk anything since they captured him. He sat up and thought to John, *"I am a poor host. Would you like something to eat or drink? I can have the ladies make anything you want."*

John replied, *"I could use a drink of water. Please have Petty Officer Smith prepare it. He knows what must be done. My dietary requirements differ greatly from yours. I must wait until I return to my people."*

Bill called for Casey and asked her to find Terry and bring him here.

She quickly glanced at the alien and went to find Terry.

While they waited, Bill asked, "Where do your people come from?"

John didn't respond immediately, but he said, *"My people come from hundreds of different worlds. My world is only one. We have been around since before the first single-celled animals formed on your planet."*

"You told us you started this world. Why?"

"Our race is mainly a scientific one. We have done this on several planets. This planet started like all the others. Over time, we changed the genetic structure of a few of the creatures here. One, what you call the Human Being, showed great promise for a civilized race of people. We watched and tried to direct the people in ways that would benefit them the most."

Bill now jumped in. "You once said that you were called home for other reasons. What happened?"

The tone in John's answer changed slightly. Bill, though he could now hear anger, *"The same thing that has plagued the development on about every world happened to us. War. There was another race of advanced people. We had always maintained good relations with them. Even in our records, it is not clear what happened, but a war between our two peoples started. The war was devastating to both sides. After eons of fighting, no one could even remember what the war was about. We began talking, and the war finally ended. That was several hundred years ago, in your time. Our two people formed a powerful alliance and mutual support. We returned to our science. After the destruction of the war, many records became lost. It wasn't until recently we found the records of your word. Therefore, we are here. To continue with what we started."*

To Bill, it felt as if this story had gone on for hours. He had many details of what happened after his people left earth. When he took another sip of the coffee, it was still hot, and he realized John had covered a hundred centuries of history in a matter of minutes.

John spoke again, *"While I was talking, I also downloaded as many details as I could into your primitive brain. We wanted only you to have these details because we decided you are going to lead the people from now on."*

"Me." Bill thought, "What do I know about this kind of leadership? I don't know that I can lead the entire human race."

Bill's calm voice came back in his head, and things quieted down. *"Don't worry. You will have many of us to help you along the way. You also have your people to help you."*

Bill asked, "What do you mean, my people?"

"When we had to return home, we took a small race of humans with us. Over the centuries, they have been developing many of the same skills we have. They have some mastery over this type of communication, but they cannot probe deep into the mind as we so easily do."

"What Race?" Bill asked.

"I believe you call them the Mayan civilization. They are an extremely intelligent race of your people. We didn't know what happened in our world at the time and thought we could continue with the experiment quickly. We settled the Mayans on a nearby world where we could still help them develop. After the war, we continued to educate them to have them join us here."

It never occurred to Bill that they would find the lost Mayan culture, even with all the strange things recently.

Bill sat silently sipping his coffee a while longer while thinking. It still hadn't occurred to him that John was still reading his mind. As he thought about when they could move out of the cave, John came back into his thoughts to say. *"Soon, we must first organize this group and ensure they understand what we expect of them and what they can expect."*

Bill didn't respond to John's answer. His concern was that John was constantly listening to his mind. He felt a bit annoyed and worried that he might think something that was inappropriate and upset the relations with John and his people.

John said to Bil, *"This is of no great concern. Our people understand what is going through your mind and we do not take offence at single thoughts. However, per your wish, I will stay out of your mind until you call me, or I need to communicate with you. Will this be satisfactory to you?"*

Bill, with an embarrassed expression, thought, *"Yes, thank you. I think this will work for me as well as the others. At least, until we get used to talking like this."*

John said nothing back and Bill figured he had already left his mind along, but John suddenly came back with one thought. *"I will stay out of your mind because I have already leaned what I need to know about you. I will still monitor the thoughts of the others until I know I can trust all of them. There are a few who are having difficulties dealing with this situation."*

Bill said out loud, "Understood. I have a need for the men's room. Do you have these bodily needs?"

John said, "Thank you, but I can wait."

He waved to John as he left, and John waved back. As he passed Casey, he told her. "Take care of anything he asks for. He is now our guest and not a prisoner."

Heading straight for the men's room, he found an empty stall and sat down to think in private. Things had been happening way too fast in the last twenty-four hours. They captured an alien, found out that all the people of the world were not dead and he was going to be the leader of a whole new human race. Leaning back with the palms of his hands, pushing his head back, he thought. "How does one deal with that kind of news?"

After trying to organize his thoughts for a while, the only thing he could think of he needed to talk to Judy. She always has a way of helping him organize his mind and calm his concerns. He left the men's room and quickly found her. Taking her hand, he said, "Come take a walk with me. There are things we need to discuss, and I need to your special touch to help me deal with all this."

Judy quickly said as she leaned towards the ladies. "Excuse me, we'll talk later."

Hand in hand, Bill headed for the stairs to go outside. Once Judy figured out where they were going, she stopped and, with concern, said, "We can't go outside. It's too dangerous."

Bill smiled at her as he put his arm around her shoulders and saying, "Not anymore. They've known about us all along. They want us because I think they need us."

Judy looked at the roof of the cave and let out a sound of happiness as she realized what he said.

They continued to the top of the stairs and went out into the sunlight. This is the first time Judy had been out since this whole thing started. She covered her eyes to block the bright sun. When Bill saw this, he scanned the area until he found a shady spot where they could sit and talk.

Judy sat there quietly as Bill told her everything John had said. When he had finished, she still didn't say a thing for a long time. She only sat there, staring at the ground. When she finally looked up at him and opened her mouth to say something. However, nothing came out. She was so stunned by what she heard, she didn't know what to say.

Bill reached out and pulled her to him. They held onto each other and rocking back and forth with her head on his chest for what seemed like an hour or more.

Finally, Judy sat back and asked, "Well, are you really going to accept this position?"

Bill sat there, staring at her. It never occurred to him he had a choice in the matter. He slumped down as he answered her. "I don't know that I have a choice in this. John told me they had picked me. How does one say no to the position of leading the world? This is stuff that men have fought for since man became man, and I have the chance to take it all on without a single drop of blood being shed."

Judy could only watch him as a talked. John continued, "I don't know. This is a lot bigger than leading a couple hundred men. I don't know that I can handle it."

Before he could continue this discussion with his wife, John called. *"Bill, it is time."*

Bill glanced at Judy, but before he could tell her, she said, "I know. I heard him call."

Bill stood and helped Judy up. Before they could leave, he held her close and kissed her and said, "Thank you."

She gazed at him with questioning eyes, but he said, "Later."

Taking her hand, they went back to the cave. As they passed John's little home, they gathered him and went back to the now speaking platform.

John sat while Bill moved to the front. Out loud he said, "Please, everyone, sit down. This may take a while." After everyone went to grab a chair or blankest to sit on and got comfortable, Bill continued. "I trust everyone has had time to think and discuss among yourself about all of this and have questions."

There was a lot of mumbling, but Bill held up his hands. "We are going to do this in an orderly fashion. If you have questions, raise your hands. When I point to you, please stand and identify yourself. This is not for John, but for the rest of us. Some people here have remained strangers and I think it is high time we all got to know each other."

Bill stepped back and asked, "Questions?"

Just about everyone's hand went up. Bill pointed to the first man.

He stood, saying, "My name is Robert. I am old and this place is not healthy for me. When can we leave here?"

John's thoughts came through loud and clear. *"It has been safe for you to go outside for a while. However, to keep control of this group until we have explained everything, we would like you to continue living down here. Once I have answered all your questions, I will leave you and you may move back into your world."*

Robert nodded and said, "My back thanks you."

This got a little laugh from much of the group. Again, the hands went up. This time, he pointed to a woman.

The woman stood and asked, *"When will we be able to see our families?"*

John stared at her as he thought, *"Yes, Lynn. Again, this will not happen until we have finished our part here. When the family's return will not all happen at the same time. It will be determined by how long it takes to get all of your close family found and what happens during the testing and orientation they will go through."*

"Orientation?" Lynn questioned.

"Yes, everyone will need to go through a similar orientation that you are going through right now. You cannot expect us to wake them up and put them back where we got them. They will need to go through the same things you are going through."

Apparently, this answered her question as she simply sat down. Scanning all the hands that shot up, Bill pointed to the nest person.

Questioning like this went on for the rest of the morning, and after lunch, it continued well into the late afternoon. Finally, one woman stood up and Bill recognized her as Susan, the lady who set up the food center for the people. Her question put a stop to the questioning for the day. She asked, "You are telling us that your people set up our civilization, yet our recorded history tells us that God created this world and the people that live in it. Could you please explain why we should believe you and not our Holy Bible?"

This question brought about more whispers between each other and out loud side comments than any other question yet asked. Others also stood up and applauded her question. Bill had to turn to look at John because he did not answer as quickly as he had been all day.

John did not move, but continued to stare at Susan. Finally, he spoke to everyone's mind. *This is a very good and very complicated issue. I will explain, however, we have been at this for a long time today and I am sensing many people are tired and hungry. Tomorrow morning, after your breakfast, I will explain how this is so. Please do not worry, because this will all become clear to you.*

After a moment, Bill stepped back out front and raised his hands to quiet everyone before he spoke. "You all heard what John has said and I, for one, agree with him. I am tired and getting hungry. We need to prepare dinner and get some rest to clear our minds for what will be coming. We will gather again in the morning after breakfast."

Bill continued to stand there while the people slowly gathered their belongings and moved back to their camps. Once they left the central area, Bill took John back to his little area and made sure Terry brought him water and that John was comfortable. He returned to his family and sat down, only to be jumped on by Nancy.

Once she was comfortable in his lap, Nancy looked up at her father and asked, "Daddy, why did everybody get upset when that lady as the question about the Bible?"

Bill glanced over at Judy for help with this question. Judy smiled at Nancy and said, "You know how we go to church and pray every week?"

Nancy simply nodded.

"Well, this lady is asking questions about our religion and what John's people did to influence that in our past."

Nancy thought for a little and asked. "Did God also create his people?"

Judy didn't know what to tell her daughter. She said, "I don't know, dear. This is what we will find out tomorrow when we talk about this more with John."

Bill added. "You're going to have to wait until tomorrow, just like the rest of us."

Nancy shrugged her shoulder and said, "Okay." And then laid her head on her father's chest, satisfied with this answer for now.

Bill looked back at Judy as she also shrugged her shoulder and tilted her head as she smiled.

CHAPTER

9

Morning came as usual, but Bill felt something different in the air. More than the usual group of people were up and already eating breakfast. There was an electrifying feeling of curiosity in the air and people were quietly talking in little groups. As he went to get breakfast with his family, Bill could see people move from one group to another and join in their conversation. It reminded him of butterflies going from one flower to another.

When he got his food, he left his family to go see John. There were questions he wanted to ask before they gathered the group together. Going into his little area, Bill sat down opposite John. He tried to think his questions to John, but there was no reply, so he asked out loud. "John, you probably already know what I am going to ask."

Quickly John replied. *"No. You said you wanted privacy in your mind, so I had blocked you out."*

Bill's head went back with a curious look on his face, so John continued. *"I could hear you if you called out to me, but other than that, I did not listen."*

Bill nodded and took a bite of his food, but before he could ask, John answered, *"However, now that you have opened your mind to me today, I know your question. The answer is no. I will not tell you before the gathering what I will say."*

Bill was forming another question about why, but before he could get it ready in his mind, John was already answering him. *"I want to sense the reaction of everyone together, even you, when I tell you."*

Bill thought for a moment and showed his understanding. He continued to eat his food.

After Bill finished his coffee, he figured it was time to get to the business of today. Before he could even move, John stood up and Bill heard. *"Ready."* In his mind.

Bill had a quick thought that this form of communication was going to take getting used to.

John again replied with a simple. *"Yes."*

As they emerged from John's area, people began picking up their chairs and bedding and moving back to the gathering area.

Bill and John made their way back to the speaking area and waited until all the people had settled. Bill started to move to the front where he normally stood when he talked, but before he even took a step, John began.

The people all stopped talking when John started. *"Yesterday, Susan asked about our beliefs and the influence we may have given to your ancient ancestors. Before I go into this area for our involvement with your development, I would like to go back a little further in your history."*

John paused, so Bill turned around to check, but John started again. *"When my people first found your planet, we found a variety of life here. We studied all the life here. However, there was one species that showed interest. We invested more time in developing this species. We manipulated the DNA of these creatures and guided them in various ways. Once these creatures were smart enough, we started teaching them. Part of these teachings was religion. We introduce the idea of God into their minds and gave them the teachings of our religions."*

Quickly Susan stood up, but said nothing. She only waited until John recognized her. *"Yes, Susan, do you have a question?"*

Susan asked, "If you introduced God to these creatures, then why are there so many religions in our world?"

John went on. *"This was very good for you to catch this, but I said we only introduced the idea of God. You must remember, when I say my people did this, my people come from thousands of worlds. We divided your world into different areas based on the representation of the science people who were here at that time. The idea of a god or gods for each area was based on the specie of my people who handled that area."*

Susan thought about this for a minute and while she thought, another person stood to ask a question. Bill wanted to say something about waiting until John had finished, but John spoke only to Bill to say, *"No, I already know the questions they are going to ask and as long as it relates to what I am talking about I will allow the questions."*

John then spoke to the rest of the people. *"Yes, George."*

The man appeared surprised that John knew his name, and he could hardly ask his question. "Does this explain why we have so many races of people?"

"Yes, George, the different species of my people supplied the DNA that was available to them. Mostly from their own sources. Although, at times, we also worked together to mix the DNA from the people of one area with the people from another."

Susan sat down, however George remained standing and became red in the face. "What gave you the right to play with the DNA of my people?"

John must have said something to George's mind because he quickly calmed down. Bill heard in his head. *"Yes, I did."*

John continued with his explanation. *"George, these creatures were not yet your ancestor's anymore that you would consider a small monkey your ancestor. My people have been doing this type of work on hundreds of worlds. We have a great deal of experience. Our work is not, as you said, play. Our goal is to help develop an intelligent dominate species in each world which will develop a society that will one day join our vast group of worlds and our society. The people of your world would most likely be well on the way to joining our society if we had not been called back to our home worlds."*

John stopped for a moment while the people talked about all this among themselves. Bill tuned to John to ask, but again, John already knew and said, *"Yes Bill, I agree. It is time for a brief break. I will remain here while you get your coffee."*

Bill announced to the group. "It is break time, so get a drink and take care of any other needs you have, and we will resume in about twenty minutes."

The talking stopped as people got up to leave, only to start again as they started walking away.

Bill went to see his family first, but BJ and Nancy were too busy playing with the puppy, so he took Judy's hand and headed for the café. As they left, Judy looked back to say, "BJ, keep an eye on your sister and we'll be right back."

"Sure Mom," was the only thing she heard as they left.

As they strolled to get coffee, Bill asked, "So, what do you think so far?"

Judy thought before she answered. "I don't know, but what he is saying makes sense and answers a lot of question our scientists have been asking."

Bill showed his agreement as he got two cups and handed one to Judy. After pouring their coffee, they slowly headed back to the kids. Bill handed his coffee to Judy and said, "I'll met you back in our area. I need to pee first."

As Bill got closer to the men's room, he heard several voices inside. He stopped to listen because he could hear it was getting a little intense, at times. He wanted to listen longer because he knew as soon as he walked in the talking would stop, but he really needed to go. Finally, he pushed open the door and, as he expected, they all stopped talking as soon as they saw who it was. No one was using the urinal, so he walked past them and began taking care of business. After a moment, he could feel their eyes watching him. He turned his head in their direction and said, "You know, John can hear everything that is in your mind. Even before you can say it, he knows what you're thinking. He returned to looking at the wall and soon he could hear all the men leave.

After he finished, he went back to his family before returning to the platform. As he watched the people gather again, John spoke to his mind. *"You should have let them continue their talking. I was interested in what they had to say."*

Bill said out loud, "I am sorry, but I had more important concerns at the moment."

John's only answer was, *"I understand."*

When the people had gathered, Bill raised up his hands to quiet everyone. When it was quiet, John spoke again. *"Welcome back. I hope everyone enjoyed the break. Now that you have a brief history about our first involvements with your people. I will tell you about my people. First, I will tell you that my people also have strong religious beliefs. As with many of your religions, many of my people also believe in one God. This is a belief the follows many beliefs in many worlds. We still cannot provide a proof to any of these beliefs, even our own. Because religion is an important part of most all cultures we have found, we gave your people a belief similar to ours."*

John paused for a moment and let the group settle again after this revelation. Before he could begin again, Susan stood and asked. "May I ask another question?"

John replied, *"Susan, I am still answering your question, so you may add to it to get the answers you need."*

Susan asked with a shy smile. "Does this mean that your people provided our belief in creations?"

John took a moment before he replied. *"We do not know how the universe was created. However, we have what our sacred books have told us. Most of which were added to your religions. This world, however, is a little different. Your story of creation came from my people and many worlds, and your people wrote it into your sacred books for your people.*

Clearly Susan still did not understand and was still unclear about the answer. However, she did not ask for more and sat down.

Before Bill could point to the next person, John added. *"Because of the complexity of this subject, I would like to answer all questions about this until it is clear to everyone's mind. Then we will continue on to other areas of concern."*

Bill scanned the group and pointed to the next person. He recognized the man as Jim, from the council.

Jim stood and identified himself and asked, *"if you provided your religious beliefs to these races of people, why are there so many different, non-God-fearing religions?"*

John did not pause this time, but answered directly. *"My species was not the only race of people working here. There were many other races who worked to develop the life on this planet. They changed your people differently than my people. This explains the differences between your races, but it also explains the different religious beliefs. Other races have no specific religious beliefs, but there were rules agreed to which only allowed these different groups to do certain things. One rule that was agreed to was that we would start a religion for each area because of the importance in social development."*

No one asked another question, so John went on. *"However, all other differences developed by human evolution to include learning opportunities, fighting between races and servitude by other races, developed after we were called back to our home world."*

John pause a moment and Jim sat, but before he could move much, John continued, and Jim jumped back up.

Bill had to turn his head to cover the smile for the leaned habit of the lawyer.

John went on. *"As for the second part of your question. We provided our beliefs and laws to your world. However, others of your races did not follow our teaching and for many reasons developed their own beliefs, again much of it was after we returned to our world."*

Jim said his thanks and sat back down.

Bill now saw Ahmed with his hand up. He smiled as he pointed to him.

Ahmed slowly stood. He quietly asked. "You have talked of the Christian Bible. What about the Muslim religion? Did this also come from your people?"

John replied. *"Yes, we are also responsible for Muhammad. The God that sent him is also the same God who sent the other prophets. These were men we trained to pass on the religious beliefs of my people."*

Susan suddenly stood and raised her hand, but before Bill could say anything, she asked, *"Are you saying Jesus Christ was one of your people?"*

Bill watched John as he explained. *"No, Jesus and all the other prophets of your world are men from your world. We took these men, and the religious leaders of my people taught them. When I say my people, you must remember, my people comprise species from hundreds of worlds. These religious teachers who taught them had many special powers passed on from teacher to student from the beginning of our civilization. But these powers all originally came from our God."*

This last bit of news started many discussions among the group. There was shouting, and Tom and Casey needed to step between a few to stop it from coming to blows. While others approached the platform towards John. Bill stepped forward to stop them as Terry jumped up on the platform to help.

The arguments went on for more than a half hour. There were many face-to-face yelling matches with a couple ending with shoves. However, before any serious fights started or people got close to John, he sent a thought out that stopped it all. Most of those who were arguing dropped to their knees. Bill could not tell if it was from pain or nausea, but it was effective. It was now silent in the hall.

Even in their minds, the people could hear John as he whispered. *"There is no need to argue. While I believe in our religion, I am not learned in serious religious matters. Soon I will need to return to my people, and others will come. They will start the training of you and your children. They will help to establish this new world. There will also be religious teachers who will come to help guide you and better explain the development of your religions through our help."*

This news brought a little stir in the group, and Bill could hear it quickly growing stronger. It didn't take long before a group member, whom Bill didn't know very well, angrily shouted. "What do you mean by training us?"

Again, John only sat there until everyone settled down, and it was quiet., in a gentle voice that he used, John said, *"This is another complicated matter which will require time to discuss. I hear many people in the group who would like to take a break to get up and move around.*

Others need to use the restrooms. I want to take another half-hour break to give everyone time to take care of their needs and clear their minds."

Bill said to the people, "I agree with John. I also need to take a break. Let's all meet back here in about thirty minutes, and we can start again."

No one said anything. Everyone got up and moved towards the kitchen and bathrooms. Some people gathered in small groups and talked a little. However, there didn't seem to be the anger that Bill felt before. Bill asked John, *"Would you like to return to your area?"*

John simply replied. *"No."* A moment later, he added, *"I would merely like to sit here and watch the people."*

Bill left, but before he got far, he found Casey and asked her to watch over John.

Casey simply nodded and went to the talking stand, where she leaned against the side and scanned the area.

Bill went to his family area and found Judy sitting on the floor, watching him. As he entered their area, he asked, "Where are the kids?"

Judy casually answered. "Nancy is playing with the dog, of course. And I think BJ is off somewhere playing with Sam."

"Oh." Bill commented and asked, "Would you like coffee or something?"

Judy stood up and grabbed his hand as she answered, "I thought you'd never ask."

They both went to the kitchen but skipped the food and went right to the coffee area. There was a basket of snacks and Bill picked up a back of chips. After getting a cup, the two of them sat down at a table to enjoy it.

Bill continued to watch the people, but Judy was interested in talking. She asked, "What do you think about what John said? Are all our fundamental religious beliefs a fake?"

Bill thought before he replied. "I don't think so. Yes, the way it was written in the Bible and the Qur'an and others, we may not be exactly correct, but only from the standpoint of who is telling."

Judy stared at him with a question on her face, so Bill went on. "I mean, we wrote the human Bible from our point of view. But it is the same story told from many worlds. If this is right, I think it gives our religious books more credence than anything else I have heard."

Judy thought about it as she drank her coffee. "Yes, I see your point. But I still don't know."

Bill leaned on the table as he said, "This is because you are still seeing it from the point of view that we are the only people in the universe. I believe that point of view is now shot to hell."

Judy merely took another sip of her coffee. Bill knew her too well to think she would outright admit he might be right, so he let it go at that. He knew she would accept it without admitting directly.

As they finished their coffee, John interrupted by saying in Bill's mind, *"I think it is time to gather the people and continue."*

Bill leaned forward, and as he stood, he said out loud, "Right."

Judy asked, "What?"

Bill smiled as he reached out to take her and said, "Sorry, I was talking to John. He thinks we should gather everyone back up."

As he started walking her back to the talking area, she said, "You know, this is getting to be a bit confusing."

When Bill dropped her off at their blanket, he leaned down a whispered, "you're telling me. Try it with him in your head most of the time." Smiling, he went to stand with John again.

As he stepped up next to John, John said, *"I am sorry. Would you like me to stop communicating with you so much?"*

This question immediately embarrassed Bill. He wasn't thinking about John listening when he said that to his wife. He spoke out loud to say, "No, John. I was not being serious with my wife. It was a small joke to help lighten what you told us today."

John replied, *"I understand. My people also have humor, but it differs from your idea of humor."*

Bill didn't answer this comment, but it made him realize how little he knew about John's race.

Bill now gazed out over the people. Most had settled down and were waiting. However, there were a couple of small groups still talking. Bill said, "Could we all please take our places and continue with our meeting?"

Everyone headed for their spots, and as soon as they all sat down, John said, *"Thank you for coming back. Before we continue to other subjects, I want to make sure everyone is clear on religions. At least the questions I can answer."*

Bill scanned the group, but no one raised their hands. Before Bill could ask, John spoke again. *"I believe George asked about the meaning of my people training you."*

The man slowly stood up again, but he was not so assertive this time. "Yes, I would like you to explain what you mean by training us."

John began. *"George, I believe you are a money management person."*

George glanced around at the others and appeared a little nervous as he answered. "Yes, that is right."

"I can say, with great certainty, that the world will no longer need this skill. My people will need to work with you and others who have no longer needed skills. We will train you in skills that this community will need as it develops."

George was now a little defensive. "What kind of new skills?"

John still showed no emotions in his answer. *"That will depend on the people from my group who will come down to make the arrangements.*

My people will go over all your schooling, interests, hobbies, and other skills and make the best match to support this community."

This idea made George somewhat nervous as he sat down. Looking around, Bill could see he wasn't the only one worried. Many of the people were pointing at each other and talking.

There was a long pause before anyone else stood up. This time it was Danny, and she had her daughter Susan right beside her. *"Excuse me, but you talked about our children earlier. Would you explain what you intend to do with them?"*

Bill glanced at his wife and back at John because this was a question of great interest to him.

John said, *"I understand your concerns, but your children will receive special training. They will learn many things. These skills we will teach will allow them to become full citizens of my people. When they come of age and are accepted as citizens, they may travel to any open planet. They will enter into any field that interests them. They can stay here and work to develop this world again. The choice will be theirs."*

Still standing, Danny asked, "And what will become of us? Will we be citizens and able to travel to visit them wherever they go?"

Again, Bill watched John for an answer. *"This will depend on many things. These rules are there for your protection."*

The part about it being for their protection upset many people, and Bill was one of them. However, he controlled himself and worked to quiet the people.

John continued. *"Let me give you an example. Most of the citizens in my community can communicate as we are doing now. This ability takes a great deal of skill. You must be able to direct your communication to either a single person or many people. You must be able to block others from entering your mind to take information from you. These are just a couple of skills you must be able to master to go out into my community. We still have crime in my community, and without these skills, you would become very easy victims."*

Danny continued her line of questions. *"Why can't you teach these skills to the rest of us?"*

Bill could hear the fear in her voice and was thinking about his wife and the fear she must also be having. Staring at John, Bill did not even need to ask. John continued. *"We have found that in almost all the species we have encountered, the younger the person is, the easier it is for them to master these skills. This does not mean that the more mature people in your group cannot master these skills. It simply means it will be more difficult. When you become a citizen, you may travel with restrictions based on how well you master our social skills."*

Bill studied the people on the floor. Most of them were silently thinking. However, Bill had a question about this subject, but before he could form it, John said to him, only. *"Ask."*

Bill had to gather his thoughts a second before he asked his question. "You say that most of the species that make up your people have this skill. I don't understand how you could still allow crime to exist in your society."

Now everyone was watching John again. *"This is not usually an automatic skill. It is one that is learned, and for everyone, there is a level of skill they can master. If a person with a high skill level can take advantage of a person with less skill, they will. Not all people will do this. Those that do will also have mastered the ability to block these activities from others. We have what you might call a police force. They are usually the most highly skilled people at probing into one's mind. They can go deep into a person's mind and almost always find the criminal activity. However, like in your world, these people have rules they must follow before they attempt to probe anyone's mind. We too have laws and for most of us, we are a very law-abiding people."*

Bill liked this answer. It made him more comfortable to realize other races have problems and laws to govern over the people.

As Danny sat down, Mike stood up to ask a question. Seeing him standing, Bill asked, "Mike, do you have something you would like to ask?"

Mike stared at the floor and shyly asked, "What will become of the rest of us? I mean, the ones who must stay here, and the ones who will go to other worlds."

Bill realized these people were now accepting the reality of what was happening and asking very concerning questions. He now took more interest in the people asking the question.

John answered. *"That is a very complex question to answer. To start with. You, with our guidance and help, will develop this world again. Your technology has advanced enough that our rules will allow us to work directly with you so that in the future, this world you call Earth will be another member of the growing galactic community. There will be much work to be done, and this is not the only community we will establish in this world. However, because of the speed with which you establish this community, it is the first to be contacted directly."*

Being the first brought joy and excitement to some. Bill could not be certain, but John appeared to like this idea as well. He knew this was probably not so, because John didn't really show any emotions.

In his mind, Bill heard John say with almost a hurt sound in his thought. *"We have emotions, the same as you. We have merely learned to control them better. In public, we do not show emotion."*

Bill wasn't sure what to say to John about this revelation. "I am sorry, John. I did not mean to offend you."

John quickly replied, *"You did not offend me. I am here to teach you these things."*

Mike spoke up again and had to speak a little louder to be heard over the others. "What will happen next?"

John waited until everyone was quiet again before he continued. Bill thought this was a little strange because others talking would not interfere with how loud his voice would come through in their minds. He figured John was being polite. As John started, Bill heard him say, *"Correct."* Bill watched the people and figured John had only talked to his mind. John when on. *"Next, my people will come down and work directly with each of you to get you set up for what is coming. This will include races represented by beings from all around the galaxy. However, they all have the skills needed to communicate with you and the training to work with everyone. Over the next few weeks, we will locate your family, and possibly some friends, and clear them to return to you. When they arrive, they will have already gone through what you are going through."*

Bill saw Susan jump up next to her mother. Before she could say anything, John said, *"Yes Susan, if all checks out with your father, he will return to you soon."*

Both Susan and Danny started crying and hugged each other. A few second later, Sam came running out of a tunnel and yelling for his mother. Once he saw her, he joined the hug. Bill could also see BJ running out behind him with a big smile.

This is probably the best news this group has had since this entire ordeal began. It showed on everyone's face. While he was standing there watching everyone, John spoke to him. *"I think this would be a good time for us to break for lunch."*

Bill smiled at John and to the group, said, "Everyone, please listen. John thinks this would be a good place for us to break for lunch.

CHAPTER

10

The next thing Bill was aware of was Casey shaking him, saying, "Bill, wake up. You need to come and see this."

Bill opened his eyes but was still not awake. All he could say was. "What?"

Casey stood and stepped back. Staring down at him, she gave him a light kick in the leg and said, "Come on Bill, you need to wake up and come see. Something is happening outside."

The kick got him going, but then when she said something about outside, he was fully awake. He put his shoes on and followed her to the stairs and then up and out. I was still quite dark out, but Bill could clearly see at least fifteen of the alien spacecrafts in the parking lot. They were lined up and sitting there. He asked, "How long ago did they start showing up?"

Casey stared at him with a shocked on her face and answered, "I was only a few minutes ago. As soon as I saw the first one, I ran down to get you."

Bill didn't have time to register all this as another two landed.

Bill heard John say, *"Not to worry. You were worried about how soon. I am telling you it is now. When your people are awake and ready, I will introduce them to my people. The first day will be a get to know each other day. Then we will get down to work to set this community up."*

Bill relaxed a little at the sound of John's voice in his head and stood up. He now realized that Casey and he were hiding behind the junk at the top of the stairs. He started laughing. Casey glanced around and laughed as she stood up as well.

Bill and Casey continued to watch the landings. There were only a few more of the crafts that landed. After realizing there were no more, he left Casey with instructions to notify him when anything else happened. He left and went back down and immediately headed for the coffee. After getting his coffee, he headed for John.

When Bill stepped into the little area that was John's, he found him in the same position and in the same place he always sat. Bill went to his usual spot and sat and sipped his coffee. John watched him. After a while, Bill asked, "What are we going to be doing today?"

John almost sounded a little angry as he replied. *"As I told you a few minutes ago, today will be a time for our people to meet and get to know each other. These people will be here every day for quite a while as we examine your people and start establishing this community. After your people wake up and complete their morning rituals, we will meet where I will talk to them before my people come here to meet your people."*

Bill nodded and sipped his coffee. There were so many things going through his head that he could not stop to think of a single question for John. It was as if his mind was frozen. As he took another sip of his coffee, John spoke. *"This is a normal reaction to an unknown and completely unexpected situation. Do not worry. You will meet with a person from my people who will guide you through all this and assist you as you lead your people into a new life and a new world."*

Bill rolled his eye at John's last comment. This was too much, too fast for him to take in. That he was going to be the leader of the entire world still overwhelmed him. As he sat there slowly sipping the coffee, John came into his head again. *"Don't worry. I have looked into your mind, and I know you will do well for your people. Also, you will have us to guide you, always."*

Bill had not considered the thought that John's people would always be here to help. He was not sure that this would be enough. However, the thought helped him to settle his mind.

After finishing his coffee, Bill got up to leave. As he nodded to John, John said, *"I will call you when it is time to gather the people."*

Again, Bill said nothing, but only left and went to find Judy.

Walking out into the common area, He quickly found his wife sitting with other ladies and talking. As he walked up, Judy swung around and said, "Good morning, dear. You were up early."

Bill replied, "Let me get more coffee. Then we need to go someplace to talk."

Judy had a questioning expression on her face after hearing what he said, but Bill continued past her to get the coffee and a quick bite to eat. When he returned, she began walking with him. They went back into the quieter area of the cave and found a place where they both could sit to talk.

Bill gulped down the food he had and took a sip of coffee before he started talking. "They're here." Was all he said.

Judy again got a puzzling look on her face and, after a shore wait, she asked, "Who is here?"

Bill smiled as he answered. "Everyone is here. All John's people. He is going to call a meeting in a little while to explain about today's activities. Today is going to be a meet and greet day with all his people before we start our processing."

Judy thought for a moment and then asked, "This is a good thing, isn't it?"

Bill sat back before he answered. "Yes, I suppose it is, but I am scared."

Judy asked, "What is there to be scared of? So far, John and his people have been very nice and appear to be helping us."

Bill put his hands on his hips and leaned forward before he asked, "You mean to tell me you are not worried about being the first, First Lady of the entire world?"

Judy quickly sat up straight and thought a moment before saying, "I never really gave it much thought. Now that you say it this way, yes, I think I am becoming a little worried."

Bill sat back and took a sip if the coffee when he heard Bill say, *"It is time to gather."*

Bill glanced at Judy as she said, "Yes, I heard him, too."

When they got back to the common area, many of the people had already gathered and set up chairs or threw down blankets. Judy went to gather their things and her children while Bill headed to the podium area.

When Bill got to the top of the speaking stand, he stopped and gazed at the people. John came out behind Terry and Casey and made their way to the podium. John sat in his normal place while Terry and Casey returned to the group. People were still milling about, trying to get to the restrooms. Susan and her ladies were quickly trying to shut down the food counter and find their place in the group. While they waited, John spoke to Bill. *"As the new leader of this world, you will be required to meet with each of the new groups as we begin our contact with them. Will this be acceptable to you and your wife?"*

Bill didn't like to speak for Judy. "I will discuss it with her, but I believe she will be ok with it, as long as the children are alright."

John simply said, "The children may also accompany you when you go."

Bill thought this would make things okay with Judy, plus he knew the kids would love it. Together, they could convince her.

Shortly, John announced to Bill. *"Everyone is here."*

Bill stepped up to the front and raised his hands. It took a moment for everyone to become quiet. He then stepped back and turned to John.

John's voice came through softly as he began, *"Today is my last day with you. The others from my people are here now and will begin making all the arrangements with each of you. Shortly, they will come in and introduce themselves to you and explain what they will do as part of the transition for you."*

There was a lot of excited talk about things happening so fast or surprise at it being so soon. John didn't let it bother him as he continued. *"Before I go, there is one last thing I must complete. Danny, would you and Sam and Susan please come closer to me?"*

Danny slowly stood and took the hands of her children and moved to the front. When she was there holding Susan in front of her and Sam by her side, John began. *"There are two things I must tell you before I leave. First, our doctors will take you today to repair your foot. Our medicine is more advanced than what Terry can provide. When you return tonight, your foot will be healed."*

John watched Terry as he said, *"This is taking nothing away from what Terry has done for you with the limited resources and training he has had to deal with. Soon, though, he will have not only the complete medical knowledge and skills to take care of all of you, but of anyone from any of our known worlds."*

Terry's head snapped up, and his eyes were enormous. He almost fell to the ground and would have if it wasn't for Tom and Casey catching him. Even then, he could say nothing.

John then gazed back at Danny. *"I am also very sorry, but I was wrong when I told you your husband would come her soon."*

Danny bent over to hold Susan, and Sam hugged his mother. A moment later, John added. *"Please turn around."*

When Danny stood and looked, there was nothing there. A moment later, a stranger came in through the tunnel entrance and stood there looking around until he found what he was searching for.

It only took a second before the children realized this man was their father and took off at a full run to be with him. Danny also tried to go to her husband, but because of her broken ankle, he came and met her halfway.

Seeing this, the people who knew Danny and her children cried. Most of the women who were watching put their hands to their mouths. Slowly, an enormous cheer went up and echoed throughout the room.

As this was happening, John's people filed into the room. At first, they stood off to the side and joined in, watching the joyous reunion of this family.

Soon, the attention of the community went from Danny and her husband to the mixture of strange beings along the back side of the room. When it was quiet enough, these being moved to an area next to the podium where Bill and John were.

Bill could not take his eyes off the creatures who were now standing next to him. They ranged from what appeared to be fur covered mammals to bipedal reptiles and about everything in between. There also appeared to be people in the group, which Bill thought about.

Before Bill's thought could go very far, John spoke. *"I would now like to introduce the people who will help you adjust to your new life and take care of your needs. While some may need to return to the spacecraft from time to time for reasons that are particular to their race, they will be the ones who will return to work with you. They will all become permanent members of your community."*

This announcement brought about a long murmur between the people of the community. This went on for quite a while, but it was Nancy who brought silence to the group.

The strange gathering also spellbound Judy, and she dropped Nancy's hand. While everyone was talking, Nancy walked over to one of the fur-covered creatures and said, "Hi, my name is Nancy. What is yours?"

The creature went down to one knee and said in everyone's mind, *"Hello Nancy, I am sorry, but you could not pronounce my name in your language, but you may call me Rosie."*

Nancy gazed at her for a moment, then said, "That is a name from our world."

Rosie replied, *"Yes, it is. Most of the people with me have names that you would have a difficult time to pronounce so we have each chosen names from your world to make it easier for you."*

Nancy giggled a little and told Rosie. "That a good idea. I like you." She then took Rosie's hand, stepped out of the alien group, and announced to everyone. "This is my friend, Rosie. She is very nice."

Judy could only walk over to Nancy and stand with her. Nancy took her mother's hand while still holding Rosie's, staring up at both of them.

Bill stood there, watching. He had no idea what to do now. As he watched, John came into his mind to say, *"Are not children wonderful?"*

When Bill swung back to John, he jumped. He didn't realize John had stood up and moved next to him. Smiling, he tuned back to watch Nancy and replied, "They most certainly are."

Nancy and Judy walked with Rosie to the food area to sit down in the chairs. Bill didn't know if they were talking to each other because they only looked back and forth between each other. Then Judy laughed, and Bill knew they were having a conversation.

John now spoke to the entire group, and all talk stopped. *"I will leave now. There are other areas I need to contact. I will return from time to time, but these people will be among you from now on. I will leave the introductions for each of you. They each have different areas they will be responsible for, but they will also answer your questions or direct you to the one responsible for that area."*

John made his way to the exit and before leaving, he said, *"I wish you all well."*

Bill followed John out and when they reached the top of the stairs, there was another person there. She was a human-looking woman.

John stopped and said, *"This is the person who will assist you in your new position as leader. Her ancestors were from this world, so you both have an interest in the development of your new civilization."*

Bill watched as John walked to the nearest craft. Within seconds, it took off and went straight up. He then turned to the woman standing next to him. His mind was spinning, and he didn't know what to say to her, and only stood there.

Finally, she spoke. "Hello Bill. My name is Abha. It is a name from my people. It means brightness in your language."

Bill suddenly realized she was speaking to him with actual words. He took a step back and quickly recovered as he said, "Hi, as you already know, my name is Bill." He then held out his hand and as they shook, he added, "Welcome home."

She simply smiled and said, "Thank you. However, I think we need to return to your group. I feel there is trouble beginning between your people and mine."

Bill quickly went to the stairs and led the way. He didn't run, but they hurried. As they were going down the stairs, Bill asked her. "Are you able to read minds and communicate with thoughts?"

Abha replied, "Yes, to a degree. However, I am not at the same level as John, and I still prefer to use words. Now I can feel the anger and resentment from your people more that individual thoughts."

Bill accepted this as they entered the gathering area.

Bill first noticed Casey had her pistol out, but kept it at her side. He then saw several men standing away from the group, who appeared to be angry about something. As he and Abha entered, Tom came out from the arms room with Ahmed. They were both armed.

Bill put his arm out to stop both of them and asked, "What's going on?"

Tom spoke first. "I don't know exactly. Things were going smoothly, but then this man jumped up and threw a chair and yelled, something about, not before I kill you."

Bill nodded and headed towards the men. He could see the rest of the group had moved to the food area and Terry was there, watching over the children. As Bill stepped up to the man who appeared to be the leader, he asked. "What going on here, Larry? This is a simple meet and greet. There's no need for this."

Bill knew Larry from the patrols. In the past, he appeared to be very levelheaded. No one that Bill knew of had any trouble with him.

The man had his back to Bill and was hunched over with his face in his hands. At first, he didn't say anything. When Bill came up next to him and put his hand on the man's shoulder, he started talking. "I was meeting with one of them aliens and it said that he was going to read my mind to find out more about me."

Bill tried to sympathize with him. "Yea, Larry, what's the problem? That's the way they communicate. John's been doing it for a week now and you didn't have any problems. Why now?"

Larry stood up and moved away from the others. Bill followed him and Larry said, "With John, he was talking. I was okay with that. Now this other thing wants to get into my mind to find out about me. What's in my head is private and I ain't gonna let that alien in there."

Bill could now understand what the problem was. Larry has something in his past that he wants to keep hidden. Bill didn't want to tell him that the aliens probably already knew about whatever it was. After thinking he said, "Alright, I understand. I will talk with them to see what we can work out. Don't worry, I believe they are trying to help, and I think we can figure a way to work around this problem."

Larry finally looked Bill in the eyes before he said, "Okay, but I don't want them things in my head."

Bill patted Larry on the shoulder as he said. "Okay, I'll try to work it out, but let's not have any more talk about killing anybody, alright?"

Larry got a sheepish look on his face as he said, "Yeah, sorry about that."

Bill headed back to the alien that Larry was fighting with. However, before he got there, the alien began talking to his mind. *"I was trying to explain to Larry about the procedures we used to determine a fit in society for each person. When I told him we would peer into their minds, he became very agitated. I tried to calm him, but his anger prevented my words from getting into his mind. However, before the anger blocked me, I could determine he has a criminal background he is not proud of and does not want it known to anyone else."*

All this was said before Bill could cross the few steps it took to get to the alien. When He got there, Bill held out his hand and thought. *"This is the normal manner in which we greet new people. As you know, my name is Bill."*

The creature glanced down at Bill's hand and held out his paw. It did not have fingers to grasp in a shake. Bill was a little perplexed now. Doing the only thing he could, he grabbed the creature's paw as best he could and shook it. He thought, *"Maybe we will need to adjust our normal greetings to compensate for each other."*

The creature laughed in Bill's mind and said, *"Yes, I agree. This will take getting accustomed to for both our people. My name is William. I understand the concerns of Larry, but these are of no concern to us. We have scanned all the people in your group for any abnormal traits. Most have dark secrets from their past they are ashamed of. This is, as you say, in the past. We do not scan for individual facts from a person. We check for the potential for this trait to reappear and we have judged that all the people of this group are stable. Yes, as with today, there will be emotions that can play into anything new, such as this. However, this is not what we are looking for anymore. Also, any traits we find, good or bad, remain private and not discussed, unless initiated by the person we are dealing with."*

Bill thought about this for a moment, then said, "Thank you. I will talk to Larry about this and see where we go from here."

When he turned to go back to Larry, he found that Larry had moved up behind him. In his mind, he heard William explain. *"I was broadcasting our thoughts to Larry as we spoke. He already knows the entire situation."*

Larry spoke. "I have heard the thoughts of this creature. Ah..William. I understand and apologize for my outburst before." He stepped around Bill and held out his hand.

William didn't look down this time, but kept his eyes on Larry as he stuck out his paw.

They both shook with each other as the people around applauded.

Bill wasn't sure how much all the others heard of this conversation, but he was thrilled with the results and felt this was a great start.

CHAPTER

11

The rest of the day went by with no further confrontation. As Bill walked about the group, he could sometimes hear the conversations from his people, but it was a one-way street. He couldn't hear what the aliens were saying. Now and then he would hear a laugh and it made him feel comfortable with the way this meet and greet was going.

During the day, the ladies opened the kitchen up and served food to his group and the aliens. From what he could see, most of the aliens could eat their food. Those that couldn't eat remained and continued to meet his people. He could see that the aliens were highly skilled at working with people who, until recently, thought they were the most superior life form in the universe.

After a while, he found Abha, and they had lunch together, along with Judy. She explained things about how the new world order would be. Bill and Judy would be required to attend meetings with the other group as they formed. She also informed him he would be responsible for forming a world government.

Before Bill could interject any objections, she went on. He would have the help of the alien culture that would be established on Earth. As well as the leaders of each of the groups from around the world. It would be up to Bill what this new government would be like, but he would have the guidance of the aliens who remain on Earth. These aliens would report the progress of the new Earth to the alien government.

Bill could only sit there and listen to her. Judy was holding his hand and would squeeze it every time Abha would list the high level of responsibility that was to be for her husband.

Still, after the alien people had left, Bill had a good feeling about all he had learned today. As he laid down to rest, a peaceful feeling overcame his mind, and he dropped asleep.

The next morning, Bill was up early, but he was far from the first one up. More than have his group was already awake and getting ready to go outside to discover their future. For several, it was the first time they had gone outside since this whole ordeal started.

Bill began his normal routine with a trip to the head and next to the coffeepot. There were not too many people waiting for food, so he grabbed a quick bite as he headed for a table.

Shortly, Abha found him and joined him. He brought her to the food counter where she loaded up with almost all the various foods that were there. When they sat back down, Bill could only stare at her and all the food.

She acted a little embarrassed when she noticed his stare. "I have only heard of the food from our home world. This is the first time I have ever had the real thing. I know this is not the same food as what my people ate before we left for the stars, but this is the closest I have ever come to it.

Bill noticed she had nothing to drink, so he offered to get her a cup of coffee.

Thinking about it for a moment, she said, "I don't know what it is called now. When our people were here, there was a drink that is still legendary among our people. No one has had it for hundreds of years. In our time it was called xocolatl. This means bitter water. I don't know if this is still a drink of your people, and I don't know what you call it now. I would love to try it.

Bill sipped his coffee as he thought about it. What she described sounded like coffee. However, the name, as she pronounced it, sounded more like chocolate or coco. Bill suddenly stood up and headed for the food area. And returned with two cups. First, he handed her the coffee. "This is what we drink now to help wake us up in the morning. I added a little sugar because it is, as you called it, bitter water."

Abha took a sip. She immediately smiled and nodded her head as she said, "This is good. But I don't think this is what my people used to drink."

Next, Bill handed her the Second cup as he explained, "Over the years, we have learned how to process this product and it is now quite sweet. "

She took a sip of this cup. This time not only did she smile, but her eye got huge, and she became all excited, exclaiming, "I don't know if this is it! The taste is not as the people told. It is way too sweet. Still, I think it might be similar."

Bill sat back down as he told her, "We have become very good at making things with this plant. Today I will find more and much better examples of what we call chocolate."

Abha continued to drink the cup of hot chocolate until it was gone. When she went back to the coffee, she got a frown on her face. She commented, "This is no longer sweet like the first time I drank."

Bill laughed, "Yes, I know. That is why you drink the coffee first and the sweet stuff after."

They continued to eat their breakfast, but after a while, Bill noticed that many of the people had finished eating. However, instead of moving outside, most were milling around and not doing anything. When he pointed this out to Abha. They decided he was going to have to steer the people out.

As Bill cleaned up their table and took everything to the trash, his people watched him. Bill found Judy and the kids, and they all headed for the exit. Once outside, they stepped to the side to watch the people come out. It was as if they were walking on the moon. You would think these people had never seen the sun on their face before.

Slowly they came out, but most of them stayed by what remained of the gift shop. Bill had to do something. BJ and Nancy took off with Sam and Susan. Watching them, you would think they were in an amusement park. Bill and Judy strolled around the ships. He could see yesterday were not all the people that had come down here to work. There were dozens more. Some stranger looking than the ones in the cave yesterday.

Soon, Judy met her new friend from yesterday, Rosie came out to meet her and they exchanged greetings just as earth people normally do. When she offered her paw to Bill, he noticed she had fingers similar to his, only her's was covered with soft brown fur.

Getting to know these people and recognize them was going to be difficult. Even Abha exchanged greetings in the earth way. It occurred to Bill that these people were here to say and trying to adapt to this new world. He thought that for them to adapt to his world was going to be easier for them than for him to adapt to theirs.

"Oh, not so, my friend," Bill heard in his head, but there was no one near him. He quickly spun around, trying to see where this person was. Not finding anyone near, he slowly scanned the people again. This time, he found a humanoid person sitting in a chair next to one of the spaceships. This person was sitting there staring at him. Bill heard the

voice again. *"Yes, my friend. It was me. Please come and sit with me. We have much to talk about."*

Bill could only stand there. He couldn't decide if he should go sit with this alien. Finally, Judy said something to him, which brought him out of the daydream. Turning to her, he said, "I need to go talk to that person over there." As he pointed toward the creature.

Abha stepped up to say, "Yes, this is the leader of the religious group among us. You must talk with him first."

Bill glanced back at the alien and slowly started walking that way. As he approached, the humanoid creature stood and offered his hand. Bill took his hand and suddenly, he knew what was happening with his people. Who these aliens were and so much more.

Bill didn't know how, but when his conciseness came back, he was sitting in a chair next to the alien, which somehow, he knew was called Noah.

Bill was still stunned when he remembered where he was. When his eye moved to his left, he saw who he already knew was Noah, who was sitting there, smiling at him. Bill adjusted himself in the chair, but before he could ask, Noah responded. *"It will be my job to teach you. What you have just experienced was your first lesson."*

"How long have I been here?" Bill asked through his daze.

Noah said, *"You have been sitting here learning for forty-two minutes. In that time, you have learned earth history from our first arrival on your planet until we left in what you would call the first one-hundred years AD.".*

Bill said nothing. His mind could not focus on what was being told to him. Yet, he knew what was being said was true.

Noah explained, *"I have dumped a great deal of knowledge into your brain. You are currently in an overload stage. I may take a day or two for your brain to sort through things. Even then, you will not have immediate access to this knowledge. It will take you longer to work through it all."*

Bill could barely talk, but he could utter, "Why me?"

Noah leaned forward to talk. Even though it was mind to mind, the physical actions were like people talking. *"John told you we have selected you to be the leader of this world. The world leaders all have the same knowledge. When the world council meets, all leaders have a complete knowledge of their world and the worlds in the Commonwealth of Worlds. Today, we have started with your world."*

Bill Set back and gazed up into the sky. He closed his eyes to think, but images of ancient earth were flooding his thoughts. He was also beginning to get a headache.

Noah smiled at him and said, *"Your brain will grow to handle all that you will learn. Currently, you only use a tiny percentage of your brain's capacity. With our help, this will grow. You will know things and be able to do things with your brain that will put you far ahead of anyone else on Earth."*

Again, Bill's head was spinning. All he wanted to do was go lay down and take a nap.

Again, Noah spoke. *"Yes, you need to go rest now. Tomorrow you will feel better, and we will talk again. I have summoned Abha and your wife to help you back to your quarters. Sleep well, my friend. Do not worry, I will watch over you."*

Quickly, Judy and Abha came to Bill's side. Judy did not appear to be too concerned about Bill's condition. Bill figured someone told her what was going on. They help Bill return to the cave and his sleeping bag. Almost as soon as his head hit the pillow, he was asleep.

As Bill was waking up, his mind was already going a hundred miles per hour.

Quickly sitting up, he saw all the people were getting food in the kitchen. He tried to stand, but found he was unsteady and reached for the wall to help hold him up. As he stood there, Abha brought a cup over and handed it to him. When he took a sip of the drink, he was surprised that it was coffee, and the way he liked it. Glancing up at Abha, he must have had a questioning expression on his face.

Abha said, "This is the way your wife said you liked your coffee. You have been sleeping for about a day."

Bill stubbed back and sat on the little ledge behind him. He took another sip of the coffee and asked, "What time is it?"

"It is almost eight-thirty the next morning."

Staring into his cup, as if the coffee had answers for him, he remembered what happened yesterday. He asked, "Abha, will you please find my wife for me?"

Without a word, Abha left and quickly returned with Judy. His wife smiled and asked, "How are you feeling? Are you alright now?"

Bill stood up and was a little more stable than before. He moved around and stretched his arms and back and with a smile replied, "Yes, I think I am doing much better. However, I will be even better with some food and more coffee."

Now Judy smiled as she heard her husband's familiar humor returning. Abha and she helped Bill to a table and went to get food for him.

When Bill took the first bit, he was amazed at how hungry he really was. When he had finished what they had brought, his wife went to get more.

After eating two full breakfast plates and several cups of coffee, Bill felt he was ready to go outside again. With help up the stairs, he emerged on a beautiful sunny morning. Bill was not interested in what was going on around the compound. He made a straight line for Noah.

Noah was waiting right where he and Bill had last met. As Bill got close, Noah stood and asked, *"How are you feeling today? Much better, I hope."*

Bill took the hand that was offered and moved to sit next to where Noah had been sitting. Once he was comfortable, Bill said, "You know already know that I am feeling much better. Also, you already know what I want to talk about next."

Because of the facial differences, Bill couldn't tell if Noah was smiling or not. However, his face had changed expressions a little. He heard Noah say, *"Yes, on both counts. First, I was being polite. Second, we will get to what you want to talk about."*

Bill sat back with a smile on his face, knowing he had called it right. Judy and Abha whispered to each other. After, she leaned to give her husband a kiss. As she stood, she said, "You have much to talk about. Abha and I are going to browse the other places and see what I can learn. Have Noah call us if you need me."

Bill replied to her, "You have fun and don't get lost."

Bill, focusing his attention back to Noah, asked, "You say you developed our civilizations and our religious beliefs? After the appearance of Jesus, you left. Was what you found when you returned what you expected?"

Noah sat back in his chair, and he appeared to be thinking about an answer. Suddenly he leaned forward and said, *"No, what has resulted in this world is not what we had planned. Our society holds many religious beliefs. Many are similar to the Christian belief we provide to your people, but there are others that are completely different. This is the same with our people. However, our people have learned to be tolerant of other beliefs and to live together in peace."*

Satisfied with this answer, Bill quickly changed the subject. "How is it that you can be so certain that your beliefs are correct at true enough to pass on to other civilizations?"

"Because we have proof, unlike your people."

The bluntness of the answer set Bill aback a little and it must have shown on his face, because Noah continued.

"When our people and the people of other races on other planets developed, the God that started them gave powers to early followers. The same is true on your planet. Many of your profits, to include Jesus and his follower, they were all given these powers. From the first to receive the powers to the next, these were passed down from one generation to the next on countless planets. Our people continued to follow and when we moved out into the galaxy, we found this same thing happened on countless worlds."

When Noah stopped to let this settle in Bill's mind, he asked, "Then what happened with our world?"

"Our war happened."

Bill tried to keep up, but was not following Noah's meaning. Noah leaned in close to say, *"Because we had to leave, and were not here to guide the followers with the powers of proof. The people in power in your world killed these followers, preventing the truth in the power to be passed down. While the words have been passed down through the ages, the power of proof was gone. Your people splintered into side religions and fighting about whose religion is correct and true."*

Bill, still being confused, asked, "Which one is the true and correct religion to follow?"

Now Noah sat back and Bill could surly see a smile as he heard the answer. *"All of them."*

This time, Bill could not remain seated. Jumping up, he shouted, "What?"

The calming voice of Noah returned to his mind, and he sat down again as Noah explained. *"In the development of the majority of the worlds we have discovered, the religions were similar enough for us to develop a civilization. As we developed our mental capability in mind-to-mind communications, we found that the God on each of these worlds was the same. We found that to all, it was the same God who created these worlds. The message He provided to each world was unique enough to that world so that we could not recognize it until our minds met."*

Now Bill got up and walked around while he thought. As he was thinking, Images came into his mind. They were images of people from long ago. He knew that what he was seeing was true. He also could understand some of what Noah was saying."

When Bill returned to his seat, he asked, "How is it I know what you're saying is true?"

Noah nodded as he answered, *"Because when we shook hands yesterday, I passed on some of this knowledge to you. I will take a while before you can fully access these thoughts, but they are there. As you sort through them, you will understand more and more."*

Bill suddenly had a thought, but before he could voice it, Noah answered. *"Yes, I am one follower from my world who has had these powers, given by God, and passed down from my brothers before me."*

Before the fullness of this revelation could come to Bill, Noah added. *"I am passing these powers down to you as the new leader of this world."*

As the fullness of what Noah said came to Bill, he slumped back in the chair, staring up into the sky. There was no real thought in his mind. Not even the voice of Noah to help guild him right now. He suddenly bolted upright and said, "I think I would like to go back to my place to think in private."

Noah replied, *"Yes, I know. I have already summoned them. They will be here shortly."*

Noah said no more, but stood and simply walked away. While watching him leave, Bill heard. *"I will be here waiting when you are ready to continue."*

Bill was so deep in thought he did not hear his wife return, but it didn't startle him when she touched his shoulder. He somehow knew she was there.

Returning to his spot in the cave, he asked Judy to make sure he was undisturbed and that he had much to consider.

Judy was taken aback but nodded her agreement to the request and left. After he watched her leave, he crawled into their tent and closed it.

CHAPTER

12

Bill had fallen asleep at some point during the night. When he awoke, he found the chamber in the cave was quiet and mostly empty. He headed straight for the coffee and, after pouring a cup, he went to find Judy and the kids. When he emerged into the daylight, the sun was low in the east. He couldn't believe it because the sun was high when he went back to the cave. He must have slept through the night and most of the morning the next day.

While he drank his coffee as he looked for his family. After a short time, he found the kids. They were easy to spot. Not that because of their size, because there were short aliens also, but because they were the only ones running.

Moving in their direction, he call to BJ. When BJ spotted his father, he came running and gave his father an enormous hug, saying, "Gee Dad, I thought you were dying or something. You've been sleeping so much. Mom said to just leave you alone. Are you alright?"

Bill hugged his son back and said, "Yes, I'm fine. Even better than fine. I've had a lot to think about and some things to work out in my mind. What have you been up to?"

BJ started talking so fast that Bill had to stop him to get him to slow down. When he started again, BJ said, "Yesterday, I interviewed with a few aliens. They were really nice. They asked if they could look into my brain, and I told them it was okay. You know what they told me?"

Bill knew what they told him. He didn't know how he knew. He simply knew. "No, what did they tell you?"

"They said I had a very organized mind, and that I had clear thinking. They think I might be a suitable candidate for future missions like this one." Now BJ's voice got softer, and he checked to see that no one was around before he continued. "They said I would have to go through many years of training and that I would have to go back to their home world. I don't want Mom to know this yet. I think she will be too worried about letting me go."

Bill had to agree with his assessment of his mother. "Yes, I think it would be a good idea to hold off telling her until you can get more information about the entire program." Bill also checked the area for people nearby before he continued. "I'll tell you what. I'll casually try to soften her up for you until the time is right."

Suddenly, the worry on BJ's face was gone and replaced by a huge smile. "That's great, dad." BJ ran off saying, "I've got to go tell Sam."

Before Bill could say anything, BJ was gone from sight. Bill was now focused on finding Judy. As he walked around the area for the first time, he found it strange that he knew the names of the species of aliens he was seeing. He knew more. He could tell where their home worlds were and much about their culture. As he walked by, most would wave to him while others would come up to shake his hand and pass on a thought of greetings.

It didn't take long before he found his wife. She was chatting with a few ladies from the cave. As Bill walked up to his wife, Susan, the lady he put in charge of the kitchen, came to him. Before she got close, she said, "Hi Mister President, or Great Leader, or whatever it is we as supposed to call you now."

Bill laughed as he told her, "Let's just keep with Bill."

Everyone standing there laughed. Susan spoke first. "I am so excited about all of this. I can't believe what they are telling me."

Bill acted surprised, but he already knew. "What did they tell you?"

"I talked with this man, or whatever he is, named Noah. He was telling us about how our religious beliefs came about. What he told us gave me a much stronger hold on my own beliefs."

Bill continued to play along with her. "And why is this? What did he tell you?"

"He told us that what they gave us for our belief is what they had from the beginning of time on his world and on hundreds of other worlds. This only strengthened what we believe in." Susan was so excited that she was shaking as she told him.

Bill told her, "Yes, I have met Noah. He is quite the person. In fact, I need to talk with him some more. Will you please excuse me and Judy?"

"Certainly, Mr...ah Bill." Susan said with a shy smile.

Bill held Judy's hand as he walked back to Noah's ship. By now, Bill suspected Noah had given him more than knowledge, but he wasn't sure. He needed a test. As they walked, he thought to himself, *"I love you."*

There was nothing. Judy did not react at all. He tried it again, but this time, he tried to direct his thoughts to Judy.

Suddenly, Judy stopped and put both arms around his neck and kissed him. A long kiss. When they separated, she said "I love you, too."

Bill could only stare into his wife's eyes. After a moment, he told her. "I never said a word. I only directed a thought to you."

Judy pulled back and giggled a little before she saw the seriousness on Bill's face. "Your serious. You didn't speak."

"Not a word." He replied.

Taking a step back, Judy said, "But I heard your voice say I love you."

Bill shook his head. "No, you heard my thoughts for you. I think Noah has some explaining to do."

Judy was now worried. "Yes, you better figure this out and get it under control. I do love you, but I don't want you in my head."

As Judy stomped away, Bill mumbled, "Agree!"

As they rounded the corner to Noah's ship, they found him standing with his hands behind his back, waiting for them. After the pleasantries, Noah motioned for both of them to sit. This time, he didn't sit with them as he spoke. *"Bill, you are quite amazing. You have found this skill quickly and quite unexpectantly. Most people take weeks or even months to get to the level you have discovered on your own, with no training at all. Judy, I am sorry that you had to find out this way. We did not expect Bill to progress this fast. This will change our planned schedule. We must now jump ahead and begin teaching you how to control your new abilities. There are rules in our society about the use of this ability and you must learn to control them to follow the rules."*

Bill felt like one of his kids, like he was being scolded for something he had done wrong.

Even though she heard all the Noah said to Bill, Jude didn't know what to make of all this. She only sat there quietly.

Noah finally took his usual seat and again was his normal pleasant personality. *"Bill, we must start with teaching you control. You have already discovered how to project your thoughts to a single person. This is only the beginning. The next thing is to teach you how not to send your personal thoughts, even as you are talking to someone, as well as how to protect your mind from someone accessing it."*

To Judy only, Noah added, *"Judy, we are sorry. We did not prepare for this. Until Bill can fully control this ability, I will block him from accidentally reading your thoughts. Will this be acceptable to you?"*

Judy only nodded that it was.

Noah again talking to both of them said, *"Judy, please excuse us while I begin your husband's training. We will leave this area for privacy to allow him to concentrate. I will have him home for dinner."*

Judy stood and kissed Bill goodbye, and as she walked away, she added, "Good luck and be a good student."

This brought a smile to Bill as his attention returned to Noah. They continued to sit there a while longer as Noah listed the rules and protocols his people observed to make this form of communications work so well. When it was time for him to practice, he, and Noah, walked through the town. Noah had him practice with drills they used to teach their children. Bill was feeling like he was back in grade school again.

During the days that followed. Bill's ability to communicate and control his thoughts progressed so well, it amazed Noah. Bill continued his thought training while taking the blasts knowledge from Noah. Each time Noah would pass on these blast of knowledge, Bill would need time to absorb it and recover. However, each time the recovery was shorter, as Bill's knowledge of the different races of people and the universe in general grew.

After about a month, Noah announced that the training was mostly complete. Bill had all he needed to know to become the leader of this world, and now it was time for his work to begin.

One morning, while Bill was having breakfast with his family, Bill felt something. Without thinking about it, he thought, *"Good morning, John, Welcome back."*

John replied, *"Very good. Noah has told me what significant advances you have made. I will be there shortly. Please have your family stay with you until I get there. I need to talk to all of you."*

Bill sent a thought of acknowledgement and told his family what John had said. To be polite, he still used spoken words to talk to his family, even though he had given permission to the aliens to train his children. Judy was also taking lessons, however he felt it was more normal for the family to do it the old-fashioned way.

After about twenty minutes, both John and Noah joined his family. When they were all seated, John spoke to them all. *"We now have another group who has formed a small society and is ready to go through the indoctrinations. We would like you, Bill, and your family to be part of this program, as the new leader of this world."*

BJ couldn't control himself. He let out a loud, "Yeah!"

Bill couldn't be sure, but from the way BJ settled down so quickly, one of the two aliens must have said something to him.

Bill asked with words, "Where is this new settlement?"

John projected a map into their brains with a mark pointing to this new group. It was in the northeastern part of China.

Noah said, *"This will be the first test of your leadership ability. These people were once an enemy country for you. They may not have good feelings that you will be the new world leader. What are you going to do to convince them you are worthy?"*

Bill spoke with words, "I have been giving this much thought. We once had a global simi-government called the United Nations. I would like to build a similar world government where we can all work together, for once on this planet, as a single people. "

John stood to leave and said, *"Yes, I have been reading your thoughts. What you are planning is very good. It will still need work, but from what*

I am hearing from other groups around the world, I believe they are mostly all seeking this. What will you call this?"

Bill stood and offered his hand to John and said, "I think I would like to call it the New Earth Council."

Noah stood and added his thoughts, *"This is a good start."*